W9-BIN-157

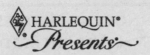

HARLEQUIN®
Presents

Summer's here, and to get you in the mood we've got some sizzling reads for you this month!

So relax and enjoy…a scandalous proposal in *Bought for Revenge, Bedded for Pleasure* by Emma Darcy; a virgin bride in *Virgin: Wedded at the Italian's Convenience* by Diana Hamilton; a billionaire's bargain in *The Billionaire's Blackmailed Bride* by Jacqueline Baird; a sexy Spaniard in *Spanish Billionaire, Innocent Wife* by Kate Walker; and an Italian's marriage ultimatum in *The Salvatore Marriage Deal* by Natalie Rivers. And be sure to read *The Greek Tycoon's Baby Bargain*, the first book in Sharon Kendrick's brilliant new duet, GREEK BILLIONAIRES' BRIDES.

Plus, two new authors bring you their dazzling debuts—Natalie Anderson with *His Mistress by Arrangement*, and Anne Oliver with *Marriage at the Millionaire's Command*. Don't miss out!

We'd love to hear what you think about Presents. E-mail us at Presents@hmb.co.uk or join in the discussions at www.iheartpresents.com and www.sensationalromance.blogspot.com, where you'll also find more information about books and authors!

INNOCENT MISTRESS, VIRGIN BRIDE

Wedded and bedded for the very first time

Classic romances from
your favorite Presents authors

Available this month:

Virgin: Wedded at the Italian's Convenience
by Diana Hamilton

Available only from Harlequin Presents®

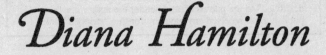

Diana Hamilton

VIRGIN: WEDDED AT THE ITALIAN'S CONVENIENCE

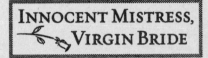

INNOCENT MISTRESS,
VIRGIN BRIDE

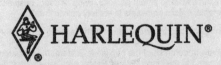

HARLEQUIN®

TORONTO • NEW YORK • LONDON
AMSTERDAM • PARIS • SYDNEY • HAMBURG
STOCKHOLM • ATHENS • TOKYO • MILAN • MADRID
PRAGUE • WARSAW • BUDAPEST • AUCKLAND

If you purchased this book without a cover you should be aware
that this book is stolen property. It was reported as "unsold and
destroyed" to the publisher, and neither the author nor the
publisher has received any payment for this "stripped book."

ISBN-13: 978-0-373-12732-0
ISBN-10:   0-373-12732-4

VIRGIN: WEDDED AT THE ITALIAN'S CONVENIENCE

First North American Publication 2008.

Copyright © 2008 by Diana Hamilton.

All rights reserved. Except for use in any review, the reproduction or
utilization of this work in whole or in part in any form by any electronic,
mechanical or other means, now known or hereafter invented, including
xerography, photocopying and recording, or in any information storage
or retrieval system, is forbidden without the written permission of the
publisher, Harlequin Enterprises Limited, 225 Duncan Mill Road,
Don Mills, Ontario, Canada M3B 3K9.

This is a work of fiction. Names, characters, places and incidents are
either the product of the author's imagination or are used fictitiously,
and any resemblance to actual persons, living or dead, business
establishments, events or locales is entirely coincidental.

This edition published by arrangement with Harlequin Books S.A.

® and TM are trademarks of the publisher. Trademarks indicated with
® are registered in the United States Patent and Trademark Office, the
Canadian Trade Marks Office and in other countries.

www.eHarlequin.com

Printed in U.S.A.

All about the author...
Diana Hamilton

DIANA HAMILTON lives with her husband in a beautiful part of Shropshire, an idyll shared with two young Cavalier King Charles spaniels and a cat called Racketty-Cat. Her three children and their assorted offspring are frequent visitors. When she's not writing Presents books she's driving her natty sports car—and frightening the locals—pottering in the garden or lazing in the sun on the terrace beneath a ridiculous hat, reading.

Diana has been fascinated by the written word from an early age, and she firmly believes she was born with her nose in a book.

After leaving grammar school she studied fine art, but she put her real energies into gaining her advertising copywriting degree. She worked as a copywriter until she and her photographer husband moved to a remote part of Wales, where her third child was born. In Wales she enjoyed pony-trekking and walking in the mountains, but four years later they returned to Shropshire, where they have been ever since, gradually restoring the rambling Elizabethan manor that Diana gave her heart to on sight. In the midseventies Diana took up her pen again, and over the following ten years she combined writing thirty novels for Robert Hale of London with bringing up her children and the ongoing restoration work.

In 1987 Diana realized her dearest ambition—the publication of her first Harlequin romance. She had come home. And that warm feeling persists to this day as, more than forty-five Presents novels later, she is still in love with the genre.

CHAPTER ONE

WITH a convulsive shiver Lily Frome wriggled her skinny frame deeper into the swamping fabric of her old dufflecoat. Saturday morning the High Street of the tiny market town was usually thronged with shoppers, but today the bitter late March wind and icy flurries of rain had kept all but the most hardy at home.

Even those who had gritted their teeth and popped to the shops for essentials scurried past her, heads downbent, studiously ignoring the bright yellow collecting tin adorned with the 'Life Begins' smiley face logo. Usually as generous as they could afford to be, because the small local charity was well known and approved of, today the good citizens of Market Hallow obviously weren't turned on by the idea of stopping for a chat or fumbling in purses for the odd twenty pence piece—at least not in this inclement weather.

Ramming her woolly hat lower on her head, her generous mouth downturned, Lily was about to give up and head home to the cottage she shared with Great-

Aunt Edith and report failure when the sight of a tall man emerging from the narrow doorway that led up a flight of twisty stairs to the local solicitor's office above the chemist's. He was about to head in the opposite direction, turning up the collar of his expensive-looking dark grey overcoat as he began to stride away.

She'd never seen him before, and Lily knew pretty much everyone in the area, but he looked well heeled—at least from what she could see of his impressive back view he did. Her wide, optimistic smile forming naturally, she sprinted after him, ready to spell out the charity's aims and efforts, and neatly inserted herself in front of him, avoiding an undignified head-on collision by the skin of her teeth, waving the collecting tin and leaving the explanations until she'd got her breath back.

But, staring up at six feet plus of devastating masculine beauty, she felt that by some freak of nature her lungs and breath would for evermore be strangers. He was the most fantastically handsome man she had ever seen or was ever likely to. Slightly wind-rumpled and rain-spangled dark-as-midnight hair above a pair of penetrating golden eyes had what she could only describe as a totally mesmeric effect.

It was so strange to find herself completely tongue-tied. It had never happened before. Great-Aunt Edith always said she would be able to talk her way out of a prison cell, should she ever be so unfortunate as to find herself locked up in one.

Her smile wobbled and faded. Transfixed, she could

only stare, her water-clear grey eyes sliding to his wide, sensual mouth as he spoke. His voice was very slightly accented, making her skin prickle and shivers take up what felt like permanent residence in her spine.

'You appear to be young and relatively fit,' he opined flatly. 'I suggest you try working for a living.'

Sidestepping her after that quelling put-down, his hands in the pockets of his overcoat, he walked away. Behind her, Lily heard someone say, 'I heard that! Want me to go and give him a slapping?'

'Meg!' The spell broken, her wits returning, Lily swung round to face her old schoolfriend. At almost six foot—towering a good ten inches above Lily's slight frame—Meg was a big girl in all directions. No one messed with her—especially when she was wearing an expression that promised retribution!

Her cheeks dimpling, Lily giggled. 'Forget it. He obviously thought I was a beggar.' A rueful glance at her worn old dufflecoat, shabby cord trousers and unlovely trainers confirmed that totally understandable conjecture. 'All I lack is a cardboard box and a dog on a piece of string!'

'All you lack,' Meg asserted witheringly, 'is some sense! Twenty-three years old, bright as a button, and still working for next to nothing!'

For nothing, these days, Lily silently corrected her friend's assessment of her financial situation. 'It's worth it,' she stated without hesitation. She might not have the most glamorous or financially rewarding job in the world, but it made up for that in spades in the satisfaction stakes.

'Oh, yeah?' Unconvinced, Meg took her arm in a grip only an all-in wrestler could hope to escape from. 'Come on. Coffee. My treat.'

Five minutes later Lily had put the bad-tempered stranger and the weird effect he'd had on her out of her mind. She soaked in the welcome warmth of Ye Olde Copper Kettle at one of its tiny tables, cluttered with doilies, a menu penned in glorious copperplate, and a vase of unconvincing artificial tulips. She placed the collecting tin with its smiley face on the edge of the table and removed her sodden woolly hat, revealing flattened, dead straight caramel-coloured hair. Her triangular face lit up as the stout elderly waitress advanced with a burdened tray, and she sprang to her feet to help unload cups, sugar bowl, coffee pot and cream jug, asking, 'How's your grandson?'

'On the mend, thanks. Out of hospital. His dad said that if he so much as *looks* at another motorbike he'll skin him alive!'

'Teach him to treat country lanes like a racetrack,' Meg put in dourly, earning a sniff from the waitress, who otherwise ignored her, smiling at Lily, nudging the collecting tin a fraction away from the edge of the table.

'Not good collecting weather! This place has been like a morgue all morning. But I'll be at your jumble sale next week if I can get time off.'

Lily's piquant face fell as she watched the older woman

depart. The twice-yearly jumble sale, held to raise funds for Life Begins, looked like being a washout. She voiced her concern to Meg. 'This is a small town, and there's only so often you can recycle unwanted clothes, books and knick-knacks. So far donations have been poor—mostly stuff that everyone's seen and left behind before.'

'I might be able to help you there.' Meg poured coffee into the dainty china cups. 'You know Felton Hall's just been sold?'

'So?' Lily took a sip of the excellent coffee. The Hall, situated a couple of miles further on from her great-aunt's cottage, had been on the market since old Colonel Masters had died, six months earlier. It was the first she'd heard of the sale, but Meg ought to know, working as she did for a branch of a nationwide estate agents based in the nearest large town. 'How does that help me?'

'Depends if you've got the bottle to get up there before the house clearance people get their feet over the threshold.' Meg grinned, vigorously stirring four spoonsful of sugar into her cup. 'The contents were sold along with the property. The Colonel's only son works in the City—probably owns a penthouse apartment, all functional minimalism, as befits a high-flying bachelor—so he had no interest in his dad's heavy old-fashioned stuff. And the new owner will want rid of it. So if you smile sweetly you might get your hands on some half-decent bits and bobs for that jumble sale. Worst-case scenario is they shut the door in your face!'

* * *

Paolo Venini parked the Lexus in front of the latest addition to his personal property portfolio and eyed the Georgian façade of Felton Hall with satisfaction. Situated on ten acres of scenic, nicely wooded country-side, it was ideal for the ultra-exclusive country house hotel he had in mind.

All he had to do to start the ball rolling was get the county preservation people on side. The initial meeting was scheduled for tomorrow afternoon. It should go his way. He had minutely detailed plans for the interior conversion to hand, drawn up by the best listed building architect in the country. Only he wouldn't be around to head the meeting himself.

His sensual mouth compressed he let himself in through the imposing main door. He was edgy. Not a state of mind he allowed, as a rule. His adored mother was the only living soul who could breach his iron control, and late last night her doctor had phoned to tell him that she had collapsed. Hospitalised, she was under-going tests, and he would be kept closely informed. The moment his PA from his central London office arrived he'd head back to Florence to be with his frail parent.

Never lacking for life's luxuries, nevertheless she'd had a rough ride. Losing her husband, father of her two sons, ten years ago had left her bereft. Losing her eldest son and her daughter-in-law Rosa in a tragic road accident a year ago had almost finished her. Antonio had been thirty-six, two years Paolo's senior. Eschewing the family merchant bank, he'd been a brilliant lawyer with a glittering career in front of him—and what had made it even worse was the fact that Rosa had been eight weeks pregnant with the grandchild his mother had longed for.

Madre's talk—once she'd got over the initial shock of the tragedy—was now centred around Paolo's need to marry and provide an heir. Her desire to see him married. His duty to provide her with grandchildren to carry on the name and inherit the vast family estates.

Much as he aimed to please her, giving her his attention, his care, his filial love, it was a duty he had no wish to fulfil. Been there, done that. One embarrassingly disastrous engagement, from which he'd emerged with egg on his face, and one marriage that had lasted a mere ten months. One month of blinkered honeymoon bliss followed by nine of increasingly bitter disillusionment.

He would like to give his parent what she wanted, see her sad eyes light with happiness, watch the smile he knew the news of his imminent marriage would bring, but everything in him rebelled against going down that road again.

Unconsciously his frown deepened, lines slashing between the golden glitter of his eyes as he entered the vast kitchen regions, searching for the makings of a scratch lunch. Penny Fleming should have been here by now. He'd phoned his London PA first thing, instructing her to set out for Felton Hall immediately, having packed enough for a few days. He couldn't leave until he knew she was here and fully briefed about tomorrow's meeting.

Aware that an ear-blistering tirade was building on the tip of his tongue, ready to be launched at Miss Fleming's head the moment she crossed the threshold, he scotched the idea of lunch and took a carton of orange juice from the haphazardly stocked fridge. After he'd left the solicitor's this morning he should have hit the shops for something more appealing than the pack of dodgy-looking tomatoes and a lump of pale, plastic-wrapped cheese that looked as unappetising as it undoubtedly was, which he'd misguidedly purchased from a service station on the drive up here yesterday evening.

Well, Penny Fleming would just have to shop for her own needs—if she ever got her butt up here! He slammed the fridge door closed with a force which would have sent the thing through the wall in a house less solidly built, then expelled a long breath.

Edginess brought about by his frail parent's collapse, his need to be with her, his frustration at having to hang around, had already made him even more cutting then was usual when that beggar had jumped in front of him. He'd have to make an effort not to read the full riot act to his PA when she finally turned up.

Trouble was, his temper was never sweetened by delay, by less than immediate and superhuman effort in those he employed, or by fools and layabouts!

* * *

It was worth a try. As Meg had said, the new owner could only shut the door in her face!

Easing the ancient Mini out onto the lane, Lily waved to her Great-Aunt Edith, who was watching from the window, and set off down the tangle of narrow country lanes for Felton Hall.

Concern for her elderly relative wiped the cheery smile from her face as she steered into the first bend. Many years ago Edith had started the charity—just a small local concern—organising bring and buys, jumble sales, writing begging letters to local bigwigs, setting out her aims. She had relied on volunteers—especially Alice Dunstan, who had meticulously kept their accounts. Now Alice had left the area, which meant the accounts were in a mess and funds were dismally low. The people carrier—bought second hand, courtesy of a legacy from a well-wisher—was due for a major service and MOT, and the Mini was clapped out. The insurance bill was due—they couldn't operate without that—and she simply didn't know where the money was coming from.

And, worse than that, for the first time in her eighty years Edith had admitted she was feeling her age. The indefatigable spirit was fading. She was even talking of being forced into closing the operation down.

Lily set her jaw. Not if she could help it! She owed her great-aunt everything. It was she who had taken her in after her mother had died when her father, claiming that he couldn't cope with a fractious eighteen-month-old, had handed her over to his departed wife's only living relative and done a bunk, never to be heard of again. The old lady who had legally adopted her, given her love and a happy, secure, if rather old-fashioned childhood was owed her very best efforts.

If the Hall offered rich pickings next Saturday's event would be a success, and the hurdle of the insurance bill could be jumped. Lily's natural optimism took over, and she put her foot down, but had to stamp on the brakes as she rounded the bend, sliding in the mud to avoid running into the back of a shiny new Ford that was all but blocking the narrow lane.

Clutching the wheel with white-knuckled hands, Lily watched the driver's door open. A smartly suited thirty-something woman emerged and hurried towards her, her beautifully made-up face a mixture of hope and anxiety.

Anxiety won as Lily wound down her window. 'Oh—I hoped—I've been here for ages. My boss will be waiting and he doesn't *do* waiting! Roadworks on the motorway, then I got lost—took the wrong turn out of Market Hallow—and then I got this wretched puncture! And, to cap it all, I left in such a hurry I forgot my mobile, so I can't let him know what's happening. He'll kill me!'

The poor woman looked on the verge of hysterics, and her boss—whoever he was—sounded foul! Hiding a grin, Lily scrambled out of her old car. This elegantly clad secretary-type had obviously hoped for a burly man to happen along. Her hopes must have taken a nosedive when she was confronted by a short skinny female!

'No worries.' Lily let her grin show. 'I'll soon get you going again.'

'Oh—are you sure?' she asked, not sounding too convinced.

'Open the boot,' Lily offered firmly. To save on garage bills she did most of the vehicle maintenance herself, and had gone to evening classes to learn how.

Ten minutes later the wheel had been replaced with the spare, and the front of her relatively smart belted raincoat was covered in mud—ditto her hands and best shoes.

The morning's driving rain had been replaced by a miserable drizzle, so she wasn't soaked to the skin as she had been earlier. But her hair was hanging in rats' tails and she must look as if she'd been mud-wrestling! And she'd been at such pains to smarten herself up for her encounter with the new owner of the Hall!

But it was worth it when she was on the receiving end of a huge grin of gratitude. 'I can't thank you enough! You've saved my life! All I can say is I hope someone comes to *your* rescue if you ever need it!'

Finding her slight shoulders grasped, and a kiss planted on both cheeks, Lily could only grin as the woman drove away, then returned to her own car to scrub as much of the mud as she could from her hands and shoes with the few tissues left in the box. But there was nothing she could do about the awful state of her raincoat.

Hopefully, her unlovely appearance wouldn't have the new owner slamming the door in her face. On the whole people were responsive to good causes. On which strengthening thought, she turned into the long, tree-lined driveway to Felton Hall, her spirits rising when she saw the stranded woman's car parked beside a top-of-the-range Lexus, then wobbling as she recalled how the distraught female had said things that made her boss sound like a monster!

But she wasn't going to back away now. She grasped the iron bell-pull and gave a decisive tug.

Having waved aside Penny Fleming's excuses, Paolo Venini had handed her the architect's folder and the other papers she needed to review before the next day's meeting. He had almost finished succinctly briefing her when the ancient doorbell clanged discordantly. 'See who that is and get rid of them!'

Pacing the book-lined study, he glanced at his watch. The bank's private jet was on standby. It would take him roughly an hour to reach the airport—less if he really put his foot down. What was keeping the woman? How long could it take to open a door and tell whoever was standing there to go away?

He had all the instincts of a high-achiever, and aggression in the face of tardiness and delay was one of them. It drew his dark brows down in a frown, which deepened as a conciliatory-looking Penny Fleming emerged from the doorway with that grubby beggar-girl in tow!

Exasperated, Paolo drew in a deep breath, about to tell his usually robotically efficient PA that unless she got her act together she would be fired, and to remember that he didn't give that warning twice. But, no doubt to forestall the expected verbal onslaught, she rushed in.

'This is Lily. She works for a local charity. Is there anything she could take for a jumble sale?'

Madonna diavola! He was beset by fools! And the creature he'd clearly mistaken for a beggar this morning looked like a charity case herself!

But he was not an ungenerous man. He gave handsomely to many worthy causes.

He addressed the scrawny, mud-stained female. 'What is the charity?'

Lily swallowed. This was the drop-dead gorgeous guy who had had such a weird effect on her this morning. He might be fantastic to look at, but, boy, did those eyes turn into shards of gold ice as he looked at her! He probably had a heart of pure ice to match!

When Penny, as she'd named herself, had opened the door and listened to her request with evident sympathy, Lily's confidence had soared. Especially when Penny informed her in a whisper that she believed her boss was indeed unlikely to want to keep the contents of the house, and one good turn deserved another so she'd see what she could do.

Lily could see he was impatient. That sensual mouth had compressed above a rock-solid jaw. He probably didn't *do* patience either!

She answered belatedly, but as firmly as she could. 'My great-aunt started Life Begins ten years ago. I help.' Encouraged by the way Penny gave her elbow a squeeze, she ploughed on. 'We help old people locally. Practical stuff, like shopping, cleaning, helping them stay in their own homes if they fall outside the social security net, driving—'

'*Basta!* Enough.' He slashed through the increasingly confident spiel. She had amazing eyes. Clear. Innocent. Honest. And the quickest way to get back to serious matters was to just let her have what she wanted. 'Wait in the hall. When she is free, Miss Fleming will help you decide what's suitable.'

Dismissed from The Presence. Heartfelt words of thanks tripped from her widely smiling mouth as she backed out of the room. But he wasn't listening—was already turning to answer the phone that had begun to ring. Telling herself that she didn't care, didn't mind being got rid of as if she were a really insignificant and annoying irritant, Lily waited as directed. She had got what she'd come for. His permission to walk away with the sort of stuff that would persuade the punters to part with their hard-earned cash and put Life Begins in a slightly more viable financial position.

His eyes haunted, Paolo ended the call, ignored Penny Fleming's 'Are you all right, sir?' and strode from the study, his mind made up.

There was only one thing to do. As always, when presented with a problem, his agile brain came up with the solution at the speed of light.

The consultant's call had confirmed his worst fears— fears that gripped his heart in an icy fist. His mother didn't have long to live. That had been the underlying message he'd picked up from behind the medical jargon. He would make her last hours on this earth happy. It was the least he could do.

And that scruffy charity worker would be stupid to turn down a decent donation in return for helping him out.

CHAPTER TWO

HAD he changed his mind? Lily questioned uneasily as, with her elbow held in a grip of steel, she was as good as frogmarched back into the study.

Had he suddenly decided she was up to no good, intent on emptying his house and making off with the proceeds in the name of some fictitious charity?

She certainly felt uncomfortably like a criminal as he curtly dismissed his PA and commanded her to 'Sit!' as if he were training a disobedient dog.

Lily's face flushed scarlet. Who did he think he was? 'Now, look here—'

But one killing flash of those golden eyes silenced her, had her obeying, perching on the edge of the chair in front of the huge desk. As if satisfied by her compliance, he strode to the other side, but didn't sit. Just loomed.

He was looking at her as if she were some previously undiscovered life form. Lily squirmed.

'Are you trustworthy?'

Taken aback, Lily gaped. So she was right—he thought she was a conwoman!

'Well?'

Of all the nasty, ill-tempered, suspicious—! Affronted now, she lifted her pointed chin, her eyes cooling to glacial grey, and gave him a dignified reply. 'Of course I'm trustworthy. I'll only take what Penny says I may. And if you want to check my credentials—'

A slashing movement of one lean, long-fingered hand effectively silenced her again. 'Take what you like. This isn't about that. I want to know if, in return for a sizeable donation to your charity, you will allow me to use your name and keep silent about the transaction—now and in the future.'

Lily's eyes widened in astonishment, her soft mouth dropping open. 'Use my name?' Staring at the forceful set of his jaw, those mesmerisingly beautiful eyes, the harsh slant of his cheekbones and the way his sensual mouth was clamped in irritation, she could only imagine he'd either gone mad or was embroiled in some dodgy scheme or other.

Whichever, she wanted no part of it! 'What on earth for?' she demanded, unconsciously aping her great-aunt's stentorian tone—the tone used to great effect on the rare occasions when the forthright old lady was displeased.

One sable eyebrow rose in amazement that such imperious volume could issue from such a scrawny scrap of a thing. A disarming hint of a smile appeared, and two hands were expressively spread.

'I don't have time to go into detail. But last night my mother collapsed. Hospital tests reveal she has a brain tumour. The operation takes place the day after tomorrow. The prognosis isn't good. In fact, it couldn't be much worse,' he announced heavily, the glittering gold of his magnificent eyes now shadowed by thickly fringed black lashes, deep lines scored on either side of his handsome mouth.

Lily got to her feet, instinctively leaning towards him, her voice soft, her huge eyes brimming with sympathy, seeking his. 'Oh—poor you! You must be so worried! No wonder you're in such a bad mood,' she declared forgivingly. 'But it's amazing what surgeons can do these days. You mustn't give up hope! Really you mustn't!'

'Spare me the platitudes.' He shot her a look of brusque impatience. 'Let's cut to the chase.'

So he couldn't take sympathy, Lily decided. That figured. He probably couldn't give it, either. And that reminded her that she still didn't have a clue what he'd been on about when he'd offered a donation in return for the use of her name. She flopped down again. Why *her* name, for pity's sake?

'My mother's dearest wish is to see me married and producing an heir to the family wealth. That I show no signs of doing so is a source of deep distress to her and I regret that,' he supplied flatly, 'but for reasons which are none of your business marriage is a state I have no desire to enter. However, to make what might well be her last days happy I intend to tell her I've fallen in love and am engaged to a woman I met in England.'

For a long moment Lily couldn't believe her ears. 'You'd lie to your own mother! How immoral can you get?'

He shot her a look of withering contempt. 'It doesn't please me to do it, but it would please her. That, and only that, is the point.'

Those stunning features were riven with pain, and Lily's soft heart melted. 'I suppose I can see why you think a white lie's forgivable in the circumstances,' she offered falteringly, not quite sure she totally agreed. But the poor man was hurting. He clearly thought the world of his very ill mother, and the awful news had shaken him. He wasn't thinking straight, hence his crazy plan.

'Listen, have you considered the possibility that the operation might well be a success?' she asked softly, pointing out something she was sure couldn't have occurred to him. 'Then you'd have to tell more lies, say you'd broken the engagement. She'd want to know why—and she'd be even more upset.' She noted the ferocious frown line between his eyes, but continued understandingly, 'I expect you're in shock after that news, and that's stopping you from thinking logically.'

Paolo gritted his strong teeth. She was seriously irritating him. Obviously a creature with the attention span of a gad-fly—veering from bristling moral outrage to saccharine triteness in the flicker of her impressively long eyelashes.

When he put forward a proposition he expected the recipient to sit quietly, hear him out and reach a conclusion based on the facts as offered. Most typically *his* conclusion.

A slash of colour washed his strong cheekbones as he spelled out through gritted teeth, 'Without the operation she will die. Fact. With it, the chances of her pulling through are slim. Fact. She is seventy years old and not strong at the best of times,' he imparted grimly. 'My mind's made up. All you have to do is agree to my request.'

'I'm not comfortable with it,' Lily confided earnestly. 'If you really do intend to do this couldn't you invent a name? Any name?'

Resisting the impulse to pick her up and throw her out, he confessed austerely, 'I deal in facts and figures, not make-believe. A real woman's name I would remember. A name I made up might slip my memory in the grip of emotion.' Not something he was overjoyed to admit to even to himself, let alone this hugely annoying creature. He shot a dark look at his watch and demanded lethally, 'Well?'

Lily took a deep breath. He was clearly set on going through with it. Nothing she'd said had stood a chance of changing his mind. And it had touched her deeply when he'd made that remark about worrying he'd forget a made-up name if he got emotional. His conversations with his mother prior to her operation would be highly emotional for both of them.

Shrugging her slim shoulders resignedly, she gave in. 'OK. I agree.'

'And total secrecy?'

'Of course.' How could he ask that? 'It's not something I'd remotely want to have known!'

'And?' Irritated beyond endurance by her holier-than-thou attitude towards what was, after all, a kindness to a desperately ill woman, he grated. 'Your name? Lily *what*?'

'Oh!' Her face flamed. He must think she was an idiot! 'It's Frome. Lily Frome. Shouldn't you write that down?' she suggested, as he just stared at her, making her feel ridiculously squirmy inside.

'No need. As I told you, I never forget facts. How tall are you?'

'Why?'

'Because Madre will ask what you look like,' he grated through his teeth, as if talking to a child with the IQ of a snail.

'Five foot one and a half,' Lily muttered, as he withdrew a chequebook from one of the desk drawers and began to write.

He slid the cheque over the desktop, his eyes lifting as he enumerated, 'Big grey eyes, small nose...' he drew the line at voicing that, come to think of it, she had a totally luscious pink mouth. 'Hair the colour of—*caramella*.' He almost smiled before inborn practicality and self-possession kicked in. '*Arrivederci*, Lily Frome.' He extracted car keys from the pocket of his beautifully tailored suit trousers. 'I have a flight to catch. Miss Fleming's somewhere around. She will look after you.'

And he was gone. Leaving Lily staring at his cheque for five thousand pounds and wallowing in the sense of unreality which was swamping her, because the happenings of the last twenty minutes were totally weird.

Two weeks later, at just after ten o'clock, Lily gave her last passenger a cheery 'Goodnight!' after seeing her safely inside her home—one of a pair of former labourer's cottages—and clambered back into the people carrier, expelling a sigh of exhaustion.

It had been a long day, following a long night spent trying to put the accounts in order. She started the engine and set off through the dark lanes for home. The usual sort of day. Organising the two willing volunteers, visiting the housebound, doing chores they couldn't manage themselves, drinking tea and chatting, driving old Mr Jenkins to his doctor's appointment.

It was worth it, though. Even if ferrying eleven senior citizens with no transport of their own to the monthly whist drive in Market Hallow's sports centre and back to their homes again was time consuming, the pleasure the old people got from the outing, from socialising with friends over tea and biscuits, made every minute special. After all, one of the charity's main aims was to alleviate loneliness and isolation.

And thanks to Paolo Venini's generous cheque—plus the jumble sale, which had raised a record level of funds—they were managing to carry on. At least the financial crisis was over for the time being. But they would have to advertise for more volunteers in the parish magazine. She and their two part-time volunteers couldn't do everything.

Shelving that downbeat observation, she wondered how Paolo's mother was, if the operation had been a success, and immediately conjured up an image of his spectacular, totally unforgettable features. He often occupied her thoughts—which was natural, she excused herself. Without that strange encounter the charity would probably have folded.

And it was not, definitely not because she fancied him, as Penny Fleming had dryly commented when, driven by something more than mere nosiness, Lily had bombarded her with questions about her boss.

'Females have a habit of going weak at the knees around him,' Penny had cautioned. 'But there's no mileage in it. He's the take 'em and leave 'em type. With one broken engagement behind him he upped and married a French actress, but got rid of her before their first anniversary. I don't know the ins and outs, but my guess is he was bored. That's my opinion anyway, because no woman's lasted more than a few weeks since then. His dumped wife died of an overdose a couple of months later, poor thing. If you fancy him you're on a hiding to nothing, believe me!'

'I don't fancy him!' Chilled by that last revelation,

Lily had protested tartly. 'In any case, I'll never set eyes on him again!'

The obvious truth of that state of affairs had left her feeling oddly regretful—a feeling that stubbornly persisted. Which was why when, yawning widely, she finally let herself into the cottage and found Paolo Venini sitting with Great-Aunt Edith in front of the parlour fire, her heart felt as if it was exploding within her under-endowed breast.

'Miss Frome—' He rose to his feet, spectacular in a beautifully tailored pale grey suit, crisp white shirt and dark grey tie, the image of the highly successful merchant banker detailed on the internet. Handsome, powerful, charismatic. And heartless?

Her knees weakening shamefully, swamped by the effect he always seemed to have on her, she got out thinly, 'What are *you* doing here?' and received her great-aunt's curt rebuke.

'Manners, Lily. Manners! Our benefactor has introduced himself to me and has been waiting for you.' She heaved her solid tweed and twin-setted bulk out of the armchair. 'Signor Venini has a proposal which, in my firm opinion, is the generous answer to all Life Begin's future difficulties. Listen to what he has to say. It will mean changes.' She smiled at the tall Italian. 'But then nothing stays the same. Onward and forward—or stagnate!'

On which typical rallying cry the old lady excused herself and retired for the night, leaving Lily wondering what the strictly principled lady would say if she knew exactly *why* their 'benefactor' had made that hefty donation.

And his new proposal—whatever it was—would have heavy strings attached. Strings her upright great-aunt would have no knowledge of! If the hard-nosed banker gave he would undoubtedly want something in return.

'So?' Suspicion glinted in her eyes, and her slender frame was rigid—until he smiled. It was like a bolt of lightning, setting up a tidal wave of tingling reaction. His impossible sexiness, *sinful* sexiness, took her breath away, and made her deeply ashamed of reacting like all those other gullible females Penny had talked about.

'We shall sit,' he announced, with infuriatingly cool calm, looking incredibly exotic against the old-fashioned background of the shabby parlour with its Victorian clutter.

Sinking into the armchair her elderly relative had recently vacated—not because he'd told her to but because in his vicinity her legs felt disgracefully wobbly—she found her breath hard to catch, because his sheer presence seemed to suck all the air out of the room. His gaze held her mesmerised as he took the chair on the opposite side of the dying fire, leaning back, elbows on the arms, lean hands steepled in front of his handsome mouth, those golden eyes still smiling with speech-stealing warmth at her.

'Your great-aunt has quite the reputation,' he stated. 'A formidable woman with admirable charitable ethics, yes? Tirelessly working for the benefit of others over the years. She now deserves to rest. Yes, again?'

The softly accented flow of words reached a pause. He was obviously waiting for her response, her full agreement. Lily pressed her lips together. She would be a fool to trust a purring tiger!

Paolo lowered his hands, dropped them loosely between his knees and leaned forward. His slow smile was decidedly dangerous.

Lily's tension level racked up a few more notches. He didn't have the look of a recently bereaved loving son. Her suspicions hardened.

'Nothing to say? As I recall, on our previous encounter you were—to put it politely—remarkably chatty.'

Gabby, he had mentally named her. In less fraught circumstances he might even have found her chatter amusing. But now she was as animated as a stone, her small triangular face pale, dark smudges of fatigue beneath wary grey eyes, her slight body, clad in well-worn denims and a tired-looking fleece, tensely held. Her hair, scraped back in an unflattering ponytail, made her look younger than what he now knew to be her twenty-three years.

He gave her an encouraging smile, confident that, as always, he had reached the right decision and that, having done so, his strength of character and dominant will would prevail.

In receipt of another of those nerve-tingling smiles, Lily felt her mouth run dry, but she finally managed, 'Why are you here?'

'Of course—the proposal I put to your great-aunt,'

he slid in smoothly. 'You may not know it, but I, both personally and corporately, donate huge sums to worthwhile charities. Now, Life Begins is worthwhile, but it is seriously underfunded and understaffed. You stagger from one financial crisis to another, and your great-aunt is no longer young enough to do much. You rely on two part-time volunteers. The rest you somehow manage yourself—cleaning, shopping, driving the old and infirm to hospital appointments, organising outings. Need I go on?'

Lily's chin firmed. Penny must have told him all this stuff. In the short time that the older woman had been at Felton Hall they'd become very friendly, and she'd told her a lot about the charity.

'You've been talking to Penny,' she stated flatly.

Was he about to offer to make another donation? Her nerves skittered. What would he ask of her in return? Or was her tiredness making her paranoid? Perhaps he genuinely wanted to help and there would be no unpleasant strings—like making her agree to be part of a lie. He'd already said he donated generously to many worthwhile charities...

He agreed. 'Yes, I talked to Miss Fleming on my return to London a couple of days ago. Briefly. She was highly impressed with what you do. But in the interim I've been camping out at the Hall and making enquiries locally of my own.'

She began to relax and feel sorry that she'd misjudged him. Especially when he went on, 'You need proper funding to pay a reasonable salary to a locally based fundraiser and organiser whose job would include recruiting volunteers. And you need a small local office where this administrative work—which I would fund on an annual basis—would be done. Run properly, the charity could even begin to expand its area of operation. This is the proposal I put to your aunt. She couldn't have been more grateful.'

'It would be the answer to her prayers!' Lily confessed, forgiving him entirely for metaphorically twisting her arm when he'd offered that first donation.

It would be the answer to her own prayers, too. She loved the work, but hated the never-ending anxiety about funding and fitting everything in, the constant fear that they'd have to stop operations and let all those sweet oldies down.

'You're very generous,' Lily said fervently, her huge eyes glittering with emotion-fuelled moisture. Then she reminded herself that she should be generous, too, and make belated enquiries about his sick mother—even gently ask if he had spoken to her about his fake engagement or whether he'd thought better of it.

'Generosity has its price, unfortunately,' Paolo drawled levelly, getting to his feet.

Suddenly he wasn't comfortable about this, but needs must. He had always been protective of his mother—even more so since the death of Antonio and her visibly increasing frailty. And his mother's needs came before his own.

'Why am I not surprised?' Her heart sinking, Lily

curled her legs beneath her and shuffled back in the chair as far as she could go, distancing herself from his smothering, dominant presence. 'I might have known you operate on the maxim that there's no such thing as a free lunch—so what's your price?' she muttered disparagingly.

'Two weeks of your life,' he came back, smooth as silk. 'As I'd hoped, the news of my engagement gave my mother great happiness. Enough, indeed, to give her a new lease on life. She's made steady progress since the operation that her consultant warned had only a slight chance of success. I firmly believe that the news of my engagement enabled her to pull through. Now, naturally, she is insistent that she meet my fiancée.'

'And you want me to—' Appalled by what he was suggesting, Lily planted her feet on the floor and sprang to attention. 'No way! Look, I'm truly glad your mother's doing well, but I did warn you what could happen if you lied!' And then she wished she'd stayed scrunched up in the armchair, because he was suddenly close. Far too close. He was so beautiful he made her feel giddy. How unfair that such a prize specimen of Mediterranean manhood should be so devious. And have such an effect on her!

She was an adult—a grounded adult—not some silly teenager drooling over some unattainable pop star, for goodness' sake!

Viewing her flushed features, the over-bright eyes, Paolo responded wryly, 'You gave warning of an outcome that fills me with joy. I am not about to regret it. Now—'

His hands parted his suit jacket and slid into the side pockets of his elegant trousers, drawing Lily's fascinated attention to the sleek narrowness of his hips. She swallowed roughly and he continued, 'You know what I have proposed regarding the future well-being of Life Begins. In return I shall want you to spend a couple of days in London while I set the ball in motion. Then accompany me to Florence, where you will act the part of a newly engaged woman, satisfy my mother, and then return here.'

'Get one of your leggy model-types to do it!' Lily shot back at him, recalling with ire the serial simpering arm-candy blondes pictured clinging to him when she'd avidly scoured the internet for information about him, driven by a curiosity she hadn't been able to control.

His fascinatingly sexy mouth indented slightly, fabulous lashes lowering over the golden impact of his eyes. 'What a short memory you have,' he drawled, adding insult to injury when he added, 'No way does a leggy blonde fit the description of a vertically challenged toffee-head. I described Lily Frome, my brand-new fiancée, down to her small nose—remember?'

Outraged by his unflattering description of her, Lily fought to restrain the impulse to hit him. The words blistered her tongue as she got out, 'I won't do it! Go—and don't come back!' Adding, in case he wasn't fully on message, 'And take your funding offer with you—I won't be paid to act out a lie to a trusting old lady!'

'As you wish.' Paolo dipped his dark head just briefly, his strong features giving nothing away. He knew pre-

cisely when to press a point and when to stand back and
wait until, inevitably, his will prevailed.

He walked towards the door, turned. 'If you're happy
to disappoint your great-aunt and let down the people
who rely on your help, so be it.' And he left her.

The now fuming bundle of scrawny womanhood
needed time to cool down.

CHAPTER THREE

IT HAD taken only one restless night for her to reluctantly recognise that by turning down Paolo Venini's offer of funding because of her principles she was being pretty selfish. An uncomfortable reality that had made sleep impossible.

When she had arrived down for breakfast, drained and bleary-eyed, her great-aunt had clinched the matter by asking, with the eager chirpiness that had been missing for many months, 'So, what did you think of Signor Venini's proposal of funding? I told him that I, personally, was overwhelmed with gratitude, but that the final decision had to be yours, because of late I've been something of a passenger.'

'Nonsense! Without you, and the need you saw, Life Begins wouldn't even exist.'

Lily had been worried over her elderly relative's recent decline into a state of fretful anxiety. She'd tried to keep their financial problems from her, but the old lady was anything but a fool.

'And without *you* it would have ceased to exist,' Edith pointed out, forecasting, 'Even with all the hard work you put in it still wouldn't have been too long before we would have had to concede defeat—I may be ancient but I'm not senile!' Sitting at the breakfast table, she poured tea and unfolded her linen napkin briskly. 'Don't hover, child. Eat your toast. I hope you were properly grateful to Signor Venini—with him as a benefactor we can go from strength to strength. I haven't felt less troubled for many months. I feel ten years younger this morning.'

So that meant two old ladies had been given reinvigorating hope—Signora Venini and Great-Aunt Edith—and Life Begins would continue to help those unable to help themselves. All courtesy of Paolo Venini's blackmailing tactics!

Driving to the Hall, swallowing her pride along with her conscience, was the hardest thing Lily had ever had to do. But stay on the high moral ground, as everything in her prompted, and she'd be letting so many people down.

Opening the main door before she'd even had time to cut the engine—almost as if he'd been waiting for her—Paolo received her change of tune without the merest hint of surprise—as if he'd fully expected that, too—and only the very slightest dip of his sleek dark head informed her that he had actually registered her words.

'Come. There is much to be done.' Moving ahead of her, his stride long and loose, he led the way to the study. Dressed this morning in beautifully cut chinos and a midnight-blue cashmere sweater that hugged the impressive width of his shoulders and the narrowness of his waist like a second skin, he was super-spectacular, and—contrarily—made her wish she'd taken some trouble with her own appearance. Not rushed out barefaced, dressed in her badly fitting cords and shabby fleece that she usually wore when working.

Vastly annoyed with herself for that unwelcome and foolish thought, she sat herself down when his abrupt hand gesture indicated the seat in front of the desk. She was beneath his notice. If she was dressed in jewel-encrusted satin with a crown on her head he still wouldn't see her.

And why the heck should she *want* him to notice her? Stupid! He might be gorgeous to look at, but he was rotten inside. A man who would lie to his own mother, a blackmailer, a womaniser, with a chunk of ice where his heart was supposed to be. Any woman who fell in love with him was doomed to bitter heartbreak or worse—as proven by what had happened to the wife who had begun to bore him!

Seated, his hand near his cellphone, his tone was clipped as he told her, 'The previous owner's housekeeper and handyman husband occupied a spacious conversion in what used to be a stable block here. It will provide adequate living and office space for the fundraiser/organiser I intend to put in place. I'm interviewing two possibles tomorrow.'

'You arranged that before you knew I'd agree to be

blackmailed?' Her face an outraged pink, Lily could have slapped him for his out-and-out arrogance—for the wealth and clout that ensured he could make things happen just because he wanted them to.

A slight upward drift of one strong ebony brow dismissed her outburst, and he continued blandly. 'You will give me the relevant details of your part-time volunteers—names, addresses, phone numbers—and I'll persuade them to work full-time while you're away. Make your diary available to me. I'll drop by and convince your great-aunt that you need a short break. A chauffeur will pick you up at five to drive you to my London apartment, where I will join you in two days' time—the night before we fly to Florence. I suggest you go home and pack.'

'Can't.'

Everything was happening at breakneck speed. Lily felt as if she were being dragged by wild horses over uncharted territory, so it came as a powerful relief to find herself able to put a stop to his dictatorial handling of the situation. She met his eyes, iced-over gold, then tilted her small pointed chin at a stubborn angle.

'I'm due at Maisie Watkins' house. She's recently had a hip replacement operation, so I walk her dog every morning and do a bit of cleaning for her. Then there's other stuff. I'll be working all day. There's absolutely no need for me to kick my heels in your London pad when I could be here doing something useful!' She almost added *So there!* but thought better of it, because he was looking at her as if she were an irritating fly that needed swatting.

'There's every need,' he countered grimly, penetrating eyes sweeping with barely veiled distaste over her scraped-back hair and down to her scruffy trainers.

'Madre is not simple-minded. She would never believe I plan to marry a scrubbed-faced child with the dress sense of a tramp,' he condemned toughly, determined not to be swayed by the momentary flash of hurt in those clear grey eyes, or the way her shoulders slumped, as if she were trying to hide herself in that awful thing she wore above a pair of trousers that wouldn't look out of place on a farm labourer.

'I don't mean to be unkind.' The words, softly spoken, came out of nowhere. Took him by surprise. He breathed in deeply, got himself back on track and continued with chilling bite. 'I do know what I'm doing— believe me. To that end I've arranged for a personal shopper to call for you at my London address at ten tomorrow morning. She has *carte blanche* to kit you out in the kind of clothes Madre will expect to see on the woman I've chosen to be my wife. Similarly, an appointment has been made for you with a top hairstylist.' He swept up the phone, dismissing her. 'Whatever else you have to do today, be ready to leave at five. You can see yourself out.' And he began to key in numbers.

So here she was, in the guestroom of Paolo's spacious London penthouse apartment, ears pinned back for the sound of his arrival, with her hair expertly styled into a sleek jaw-length bob, two horrendously expensive suitcases packed with horrendously expensive designer gear which had been virtually forced on her at the side of the bed, and his jibe about her looking like a scrubbed-faced child with the dress sense of a tramp still rankling.

What woman would go out made-up to the nines and wearing her best gear to walk a big unruly dog, wash floors and clean windows and stuff? Or were the women who entered the rarefied atmosphere of his life always perfectly groomed, elegantly attired—looking decorative their only justification for taking up space on the planet? Probably!

Her heart jumped as her straining ears caught the sound of footfalls. He'd arrived.

It was a big apartment, all polished hardwood floors, stark white walls and the minimum of furniture. Leather and steel stuff, nothing in the way of softness. Not at all homey—like the man himself.

Her heart-rate quickened as she heard him draw closer. He was pausing outside her room now.

A tap on the door.

She resisted the impulse to scramble beneath the feather-light duvet and pretend to be asleep, because she wasn't a coward and he was only human.

She watched him enter. Formidably handsome, dressed in a dark grey business suit, he was every inch the incredibly wealthy banker—one of the world's movers and shakers. She had to remind herself he was also a heartless womaniser who only had to flick a finger to have the world's most beautiful females flocking, each and every one of them believing she could hold his interest for longer than the last, each and every one of them getting the elbow when coming up against his low boredom threshold. And his boredom was utterly inevitable according to Penny Fleming, who should know.

'*Madonna diavola!* Do you have to look like a terrified rabbit?' Broad shoulders rigid, he strode into the room. If his supposed future wife was going to look as if the devil himself had come to get her every time she saw him, then the deception that was necessary to his mother's continued good progress was dead in the water!

She'd wondered if he would notice her new hairstyle and comment. Of course he hadn't. All he'd noticed about her was her resemblance to a rabbit! 'You spook me!' she confessed on a mumble, pulling the edges of the swamping bathrobe she'd found in the *en suite* bathroom closer together.

'I? In what way?'

He looked genuinely puzzled, brows drawing together above those spectacular golden eyes, so she told him. 'You're like a steamroller squashing an ant. You want something. You get it. Never mind the objections of lesser beings! Feeling like an ant in your way is not fun.'

His expressive mouth twisted wryly. 'I see.'

Not used to tiptoeing around the finer feelings of his employees, because they were paid handsomely to perform their duties and were well used to jumping when he said jump, he had seen no reason to treat Lily Frome any differently.

She—or her charity—was being paid to act the part of his fiancée for a short while, which, logically, made her his employee. But her reaction to him told him he was going to have to tread more carefully in what he could now see was a delicate situation. He must get her on board or the deception would fall flat on its face.

'I'll have to take care to make a detour around any ant that gets in my way.'

His slow smile was pure magic. Lily shivered. She hated the way he could affect her but, annoyingly, she didn't seem able to do anything about it.

On the whole it was better for her equilibrium when he simply barked out his orders and dismissed her, she decided wretchedly. And when he asked, 'Have you eaten?' all she could do was dumbly shake her head.

'Good.' That heartbreaker smile flashed again. 'I've ordered takeaway.' He advanced, held out his hand. 'Come.'

Looking pointedly away from that outstretched hand, because the temptation to slide her own into its lean, strong warmth was really intense, Lily muttered, 'Not hungry,' just as her empty stomach gave a betraying growl of protest. 'And I'm not dressed,' she added for good measure.

Carefully holding onto his patience, Paolo countered, smooth as cream, 'Come as you are. It's not a party! Besides, we need to talk. We've an early start, so it's now or never, because I shall have to work on the flight out.'

He would think she was behaving ridiculously, Lily conceded. And she was. Ignoring his hand, she slid her legs out of the bed and made sure she was decently covered by the huge bathrobe. Lifting the skirts so she didn't trip over the trailing length, she followed him out of the room and gave herself a pep talk.

Theirs was a business arrangement—a shady business arrangement, she reminded herself forcefully. She'd agreed to go along with it despite her reservations, so it was time she started to behave like an adult around him. They would have to talk things over—she certainly needed to know if the part-timers had proven willing to take over her work while she was away—and she was going to have to make herself stop having these attacks of juvenile silliness every time she looked at him.

Trouble was, he had the sort of magnetic sex appeal she had never encountered before, and that, combined with his staggering male beauty, was potent stuff. But she could discount that. Of course she could. Hormones and lust. What she knew of his character was more than enough to put those two evils back in their boxes.

As they approached the glass-topped table in the dining area, a uniformed waiter appeared from the clinically sterile kitchen. Another followed, pushing a trolley, and the table was already laid with silverware and sparkling crystal.

Lily's eyes widened. This was Paolo's idea of a takeaway?

The sudden and hastily suppressed urge to giggle made her feel as if her lungs were about to burst. For her, a takeaway was a rare treat consisting of cod and chips in a warm, greasy package, or foil cartons of sweet and sour chicken and fried rice from the local Chinese restaurant.

This—giant prawns with a delicate lemon sauce, slices of meltingly tender venison on a bed of wild mushrooms, a syllabub to die for—was obviously a wealthy man's idea of a takeaway!

Too busy enjoying every mouthful, and reflecting on how the other half lived, Lily forgot the deceitful part she was expected to play during the coming two weeks for long enough to relax and ask, 'Why champagne?' She'd only tasted it once before, at a friend's wedding, and hadn't liked it. So this had to be something special because she'd already got through two glasses.

'To celebrate the start of—' He'd been about to say *Our hopefully brief association* but, recalling her rather thin skin, substituted 'Of our mutually satisfactory business arrangement.'

He was leaning back in his seat and his eyes were gleaming in an almost sultry way, she registered, with a strange and unwelcome inner flutter, coming straight back down to earth with a thump.

She put her champagne flute down on the table with a clatter. 'I don't feel like celebrating. Not when our so-called business arrangement is based on a whopping lie.'

'A white lie aimed to please a frail elderly lady,' he reminded her, careful not to snap, as was his inclination when his judgement was questioned. 'And you might be interested to hear that a certain Kate Johnson will be in place at the charity by the end of the month. She will take care of fundraising and day-to-day organisation. She has impeccable references, having worked as a fund-raiser for a well-known charity based in Birmingham. Also, substantial funds have been placed in the charity's account,' he completed with cool precision.

The slightest dip of his head brought the waiter gliding forward to receive his instruction that coffee would be taken in the living room.

Squashed again, Lily recognised, as he escorted her through. The slightest hint of criticism flattened as he rolled over her with his reminders of what Life Begins would be gaining at his no doubt vast expense.

'May I suggest,' he drawled, as he watched with con-cealed amusement as she tried to perch on the edge of the slippery surface of the leather sofa and control the wayward swamping folds of the vastly over-large robe she was wearing, 'that for the next two weeks we pull together, not in different directions? As far as my mother is concerned we are engaged to be married. She will expect us to behave as lovers—and I hope you will try—but if you can't manage that you must act as if I am at the very least your friend and not your enemy.'

Lily's face flamed. Act as if they were lovers? The very thought made her heart beat so fast she was sure it would leap out of her chest. He could take that preposterous suggestion and bury it deep in the nearest dustbin!

Thankfully, she was spared the need to give an immediate answer by the arrival of the coffee tray and Paolo's final dismissal of the waiter.

Stealing a look at him from beneath tangled lashes, she felt her tummy flip alarmingly. It was so unfair! Just look at him—every inch the powerful alpha male, sophisticated, breathtakingly wealthy and staggeringly good to look at. Sexy. In spades. She could have coped much better if he'd been fat and bald with the sex appeal of a frog!

Clamorous warning bells had rung at the prospect of even *pretending* to be his lover. For him it would be tongue-in-cheek play-acting, but for her it would be too dangerous to contemplate.

Even before the waiter had closed the door behind him, she blurted, 'This scam you've dreamed up can't work! For a start, friends don't trample on each other, treat each other as if their opinions are worthless. So it will be really difficult to pretend you're my friend!'

He'd taken a chair on the opposite side of the low coffee table. He poured dark, hot coffee into small goldrimmed cups, his movements deft and economical, and conceded, 'I see your point. However, now matters are arranged, everything smoothly in place, it will be different—I promise.'

In all areas of his life, business and personal, he made decisions and acted on them, allowing nothing to get in his way. Using persuasion to counter an objecting voice was unusual for him, but with so much at stake he had to grit his teeth, keep his temper, and *try*.

He smiled. The slow, sexy smile that dazzled her eyes and set her pulses racing.

'If you have an opinion, and it is valid, it will be listened to.'

Big of him! 'Does there always have to be a caveat?' She accepted the cup he offered. Whatever opinion she offered he was bound to say it wasn't valid!

'*Scusi!*' He flashed her a disarming grin and relaxed back in his chair. When she wasn't regarding him as the devil incarnate she could be amusing company. Come to think of it, he might enjoy moulding this stubborn, unremarkable scrap of female opposition to his will. Brilliant eyes assessed her thoroughly. Maybe she wasn't quite as unremarkable as he'd thought. 'The new hairstyle suits you perfectly. Pretty.'

He caught the surprise in those big grey eyes before she looked quickly away, her pale skin pinkening, and to his own amazement he found he felt ashamed of himself. He hadn't been treating her like a human being with feelings that could be hurt—or completely squashed, as she'd accused.

Her hands—delicate, fine-boned, small hands, he noted for the first time—were unsteady as she replaced her cup on its saucer. And, realising it was time to quit while he was ahead, he said gently, 'Goodnight, Lily. It's late and we have an early start. Sleep well.'

He watched with veiled satisfaction as she scrambled

to her feet and exited in swamping folds of out-of-control bathrobe.

Tread softly, a little gentle flattery, and the next two weeks would be sailed through with no problems at all.

CHAPTER FOUR

As SHE boarded the Venini private jet, with Paolo's hand lightly insistent on the small of her back—a reminder, as if she needed one, that it was now far too late to back out—Lily felt seriously light-headed. Partly nerves at the prospect of what lay ahead of her—her role in a distasteful deception—and partly, she had to be honest, because Paolo was being *nice* to her.

She'd gone to bed with his compliment about her new hairstyle throbbing in her ears and heating her skin, totally amazed that he had actually noticed something positive about her appearance.

She could have got over that, of course she could, but then the way his eyes had registered stunned approval when she'd presented herself early this morning, wearing the wickedly expensive cream-coloured linen suit and heeled sandals that she'd selected to travel in from the clothes that had been picked out for her, had really knocked her for six.

Especially when he'd moved right up to her and tilted

her chin, producing a clean white handkerchief and gently wiping away the scarlet lipstick she'd taken such pains to apply.

At the touch of his cool, lean fingers, the gentle movement of the fabric against her lips, every sane thought had flown right out of her head.

His eyes, veiled by thick dark lashes, had been intent on what he was doing, his beautiful mouth just slightly smiling, and every inch of her suddenly tense body had craved to move closer to the dominating male strength of his. She had nearly fainted with the urgent throbbing of every cell in her body when he'd run a finger softly over her parted lips and imparted, in a tone that was thicker and deeper than she had heard before, 'You have a lovely mouth. Soft and incredibly lush. Pink and inviting. It's a sin to cover it with screaming scarlet.'

'Inviting.' What did *that* mean? That he'd wanted to kiss her? Her heart had begun to pound and clatter; her breathing had grown ragged.

She'd gulped.

With a feeble effort, which he could have stayed with the tip of one finger, she had forced herself to twist away from the sheer temptation of him.

Of course he hadn't wanted to kiss her! As if! It was completely obvious what he'd been doing.

She could pinpoint exactly when he had started to treat her like a living, breathing female. Right after she'd told him she couldn't even begin to treat him as if he were a friend when all he did was trample on her.

Paolo Venini was turning on the charm solely in the hope of making her more compliant—she could see straight through him!

Even so, her tummy muscles clenched now as he leaned over and fastened her seat belt for her. She could see every pore of his olive-toned skin, the darkly shadowed jawline, the gleam of those brilliant eyes. She breathed in the mineral tang of the aftershave he used and felt giddy.

He was so dangerous!

But only if she allowed him to be, she reminded herself sternly. And she wouldn't! She could be strong enough to ignore all that overcharged sexual charisma.

As the plane taxied down the runway she consoled herself with that heartening thought, and when they were airborne, made haste to release her seat belt to stop him moving up close and doing it for her. When he half turned in his seat, angled towards her, she was as proud as if she had just won an Olympic medal when she managed casually, coolly, 'You said you wanted to work. Please go ahead. I'm not about to disturb you and hurl objections at you at this late stage.'

'I'm relieved to hear it.'

Warmth in his voice—a smile, even. Nerves prickling, Lily kept staring straight ahead. Looking at him always caused her problems.

Her profile was a delight. Long lashes veiling those big grey eyes, neat nose just slightly pinched around the nostrils, lush lips clamped together. A sign of her apprehension? Compassion stirred within him for the first time. She didn't like the situation he'd dragooned her into, and it was up to him to try to smooth the way for her.

There had been other firsts, too, he recognised in retrospect. Like noticing the flattering new hairstyle that framed her kittenish face. And then this morning he'd been actually stunned by a woman's appearance— something that had never happened before. Without the workmanlike trousers and shapeless tops the skinny kid had been revealed as a delightful pocket-sized Venus. The expertly tailored suit she had chosen to wear to travel in skimming small but perfectly formed breasts, emphasising a tiny, tiny waist and showing off the very female curve of her hips.

A glow of what could only be pride in his achievement coursed heatedly through his veins. *He* had brought about this startling transformation, and Madre would have no trouble believing that this was the woman he had chosen to be his wife.

Faint colour touching his slanting cheekbones, he reached into an inner pocket. Her head was turned away. She was staring out at the clouds. He touched her arm and she stiffened. Wary. Like a kitten who didn't know where the next kick was coming from.

His strong, dark features clenched. *Madre di Dio!* Had he, through the force of his character, treated her so badly? Things would have to change. His parent was strongly moralistic, sheltered, strictly reared, and she deplored what she called the laxness of the younger generation, but even she would expect a newly engaged couple to touch each other!

'Lily.' Her name, falling softly from his lips, gained her attention. She turned, her eyes wide. He took her hand and felt her tense. 'Wear this.' As he slid the ring onto her wedding finger Lily flinched, a shiver running right down her rigid spine and back up again as he imparted warmly, 'It has been passed down through generations of Venini brides. Madre will expect to see you wearing it.'

The diamond was simply huge, set in antique gold and surrounded by cabochon-cut sapphires. A fabulously expensive prop for a horribly cheap deception! Everything inside her rebelled afresh.

Firmly dismissing the frisson she'd experienced when the mind-bogglingly handsome and wickedly sexy Paolo Venini had placed the ring on her finger, she cast around for some objection he would go for—because her real one would cut no ice with a man who didn't appear to have a conscience and always thought he was right.

'It's much too big. I can't wear it. I'd only lose it, and it's got to be worth a fortune,' she got out as she attempted to remove the ring which symbolised their sham engagement.

His large, lean hands closed over hers. 'I'll have it made smaller.' Like the rest of her, her hands were tiny, her fingers long and slender. Amazingly, feeling them beneath his own much larger hands made him feel quite urgently protective.

'You can't do that,' Lily pointed out blithely, doing her utmost to ignore the way his skin burned against hers. 'I know you don't want to marry right now. But one day you will. And then you'll have to have it altered back again, to fit a bigger finger.'

Incisive golden eyes held hers, his sensual mouth curving as he countered teasingly. 'I would never marry a woman with fat fingers! Wear it for the time being. Once she has seen it on your finger I'll tell my mother it has to be altered. I know what I'm doing, believe me.'

He still held her hand. When she tried to pull away his grip merely tightened. Rivers of sensation racing through her made her feel weirdly distracted, and she struggled to focus before she finally managed earnestly, 'I don't think you do—know what you're doing. Not really. Think about it. How long can an engagement last? A couple of years? Ten? Some time you're going to have to tell her the whole thing's off. Then how will she feel? Really disappointed because her hopes of seeing you settled and giving her grandchildren have come to nothing!'

He withdrew his hand. Lily felt the coldness settle over him, and his features were bleak as he incised brittly, 'I would be overjoyed if I believed that Madre had two years left to her.' Turning away, he reached for the briefcase that held his work, completely dismissing her and the conversation.

But Lily, once her easily touched sympathies had been engaged, wasn't prepared to accept his dismissal.

The poor man was dreadfully worried about his mother, and despite the successful outcome of her operation he was still of the opinion that she wouldn't survive very long. Wriggling round in her seat to face him squarely, she said gently, 'You love your mother very much, don't you?'

'Naturally.' The word held a bite.

So the hard nut did have a soft centre. Prepared to explore the phenomenon, to understand him better and forgive his sin of coercion, she pressed, 'And you'd do anything to make her happy?'

'That is what this is all about.' Briefcase abandoned, he slewed round to face her, his eyes derisive. 'Don't tell me you'd forgotten? You can't imagine I'm going through this charade for the pleasure of your company!'

As soon as the words were out Paolo regretted them. She looked as if she had just received a slap in the face. But he had spoken the absolute truth, and if her feelings were hurt, tough. He was not in the habit of stepping softly around the feelings of employees who were being paid handsomely to do as he required—and Lily Frome and her charity were being paid far more handsomely than most.

With a slight shrug of wide, immaculately suited shoulders, Paolo lifted the briefcase again and settled down to work.

Apart from explaining that for the duration of her recuperation his mother was staying with her nurse and companion at the family villa in the hills beyond

Florence, Paolo remained silent as he drove a sleek Ferrari through the unspoiled Tuscan countryside.

She might as well be invisible, Lily decided, and told herself she didn't care. Being ignored was absolutely better than when he was being nice, because when he complimented her, smiled at her or took her hand she, to her shame, went all gooey inside, and promptly forgot what a manipulative creep he was. He might have a slightly redeeming soft spot where his parent was concerned, but beneath that stunning packaging he was mostly just bad-tempered, impatient, arrogant and devoid of conscience. He might have a brilliant brain when it came to business, but he was happy to ride roughshod over the feelings of those he considered to be his inferiors.

That assessment planted firmly in her mind, she told herself that she had to remember that Life Begins would benefit immensely from his funding. Her great-aunt would sleep easier, and she, when this was over, would work hard and try to forget the part she had played in the charity's salvation.

As for the next two weeks—well, she would get through it as best she could. And maybe, if she presented herself as the sort of woman Signora Venini wouldn't welcome into her family, the poor thing wouldn't be at all upset when her hateful son told her the engagement was off! She'd be mightily relieved!

She could pretend to be a complete bitch—cold, hard, only showing any animation when asking how much Paolo was worth—or she could be a complete boor—talking with her mouth full, shrieking with raucous laughter at nothing in particular, scratching herself and burping. Deciding which gave her a heady feeling of control, of paying him back for forcing her to do this.

She must have been grinning at the possible scenarios, because he gave her a sharp look that wiped the smile from her face as he said, 'We're here,' and swung the powerful car between two immense security gates that swung open at his approach.

The wide, curving drive was bordered by tall cypresses which banded the fine-gravelled surface with deep shadows, and Lily's amusing mental pictures vanished, leaving her feeling deeply apprehensive. This was serious, and she knew that there was no way she could attempt to act the part of this intimidating man's fiancée and change her character at the same time!

Her heart taking residence in her shoes, she watched as the immense white-stuccoed villa came into view. Large windows glittered in the afternoon sun, and giant stone urns filled with colourful flowers flanked the shallow flight of steps that led up to the main door.

One cue, the door opened, and a slim, white-jacketed servant hurried towards the car as it slid to a halt. Exiting, Paolo spoke in his own language. The only words Lily could pick out were references to his mother, as she sat in her seat like an overlooked package.

The imposing villa was completely intimidating. A

palace fit only for the rarefied and screamingly wealthy. How could she, an ordinary, dirt-poor charity worker, hope to even *pretend* to fit in? For the millionth time she wished she'd never agreed to this. Just gritted her teeth and struggled on as best she could.

When Paolo strode round to her side of the car, opened the door and extended his hand to help her out, all she wanted to do was screw herself down in her seat and refuse to budge.

His manufactured tender smile tightened. He must have seen the mutiny on her face, Lily recognised, and she released a pent-up breath, reluctantly accepting his assistance. After all, she had made a bargain with this devil in heart-throb's clothing, and she didn't go back on her word, so annoying him would get her nowhere.

'Mario will take your luggage up to your room.' His arm was around her small waist. 'I suggest you freshen up while I greet my mother. And try to remember that we're supposed to be head over heels in love with each other.'

A statement guaranteed to make her stomach turn over and set her knees trembling.

His strong arm around her was the only thing keeping her upright, Lily realised as he steered her towards the imposing entrance. Her legs had gone completely tottery, and a million butterflies were having a ball in her tummy. She could only manage a wavery smile as he introduced her to a smiling middle-aged lady.

'Agata is my housekeeper. She has excellent English. Apply to her for anything you need for your comfort.'

His smile broadened, the arm around her waist drawing her closer. Lily shuddered in reaction. 'She will show you to your room, *cara*. I will come for you in a short while.'

He was really getting into character, Lily grumbled to herself as she followed Agata's broad back up the wide sweeping staircase—even dredging up an endearment for the benefit of his housekeeper. Deception must come easily to him. In the play-acting stakes she would come a very poor second!

As the ornate staircase branched in two directions they veered left, and on the first landing Agata flung open the first door they came to. 'Your room, *signorina*. You like?'

How could she confess that the vast, opulent room intimidated her when those kindly dark eyes were smiling into her own?

'It's beautiful, Agata, thank you.'

Her luggage already stood at the foot of the enormous canopied bed. Spirited up by means of some discreet servants' staircase, she guessed, and could only widen her eyes in wonderment when the housekeeper stated comfortably, 'The English tea will be brought to you immediately. Donatella will unpack for you, and if there's anything else you require then you must please ring for me.' She left before Lily could gather her wits together to protest that she didn't want to be any trouble.

So this was how the other half lived, she thought uneasily as she edged gingerly over the thick-piled cream-coloured carpet towards the row of tall windows—louvred and ornately draped—that marched along the length of one ivory-coloured wall. Surrounded by luxury, good taste and the trappings of vast wealth, with servants to cater to one's every whim and no need to lift a finger.

The panoramic view over manicured gardens to the rolling Tuscan countryside was truly magnificent, and she was lost in admiration when a pretty Italian girl bearing a tea tray entered after a deferential knock.

'*Signorina…*' The girl placed the tray on a low table beside a silk-upholstered armchair, her brown eyes curious as they swept Lily's diminutive figure—no doubt checking out her probable future mistress, Lily realised, feeling decidedly queasy.

'Thank you,' she said, although tea was the last thing she wanted. Her stomach would reject anything she tried to put into it. But she sank obediently into the chair and poured the tea, her hand shaking. Someone had gone to the trouble to make it, and this poor girl had struggled up all those stairs with it, so she had to make an effort.

Nevertheless, the sight of the maid opening her suitcases was enough to get Lily to her feet again, protesting, 'Look—there's no need, really. I can do that myself. It's no trouble.'

But the maid obviously had no English. She just looked up anxiously, and Lily felt foolish and about two inches tall. The young Italian girl would take unpacking for guests as completely normal—part of what she was hired to do. Having a crazy foreigner gabbling at her in a language she didn't understand would make her feel as if she were doing something wrong. Lily was going to have to remember that she'd entered a world that was totally different from her own.

'Sorry.' Her face pink with embarrassment, Lily backed away limply. Desperate to escape without daubing more egg on her face, she headed for a door she'd noticed set between the vast wardrobe and an antique dressing table.

Confronted by an elegantly proportioned bathroom, complete with a huge marble bath, a shower unit, and enough fluffy towels to serve a rugby team, she kicked off her shoes, deciding that the shower would make the perfect hiding place. Just until she had got her head around the uncomfortable feeling that she was way out of her depth.

Carefully placing the unwanted and over-large engagement ring on the marble top of the vanity unit, she stripped off and scurried into the shower. She stayed there, pounded by hot water, wondering how long it would take Donatella to finish unpacking and remove herself, leaving her with the solitude she would need to get herself into the right frame of mind for the dreaded first meeting with the poor woman she was about to so cruelly dupe. She wondered nervously how she would cope when Paolo played his role, as promised, and treated her as if she were the love of his life. Go to pieces, probably! She'd never deceived anyone, and didn't know how she was going to do it.

'*Porca miseria!* No one takes a shower for an hour! Do you intend to boil yourself?'

Mortification followed shock as Lily peered through the steam at one clearly aggravated Italian male. His sharp suit jacket was soaked, where he'd flung open the glass door and reached in to cut off the flow of water, and his sharp tongue was in evidence as he ordered, 'Get dressed! My mother is anxious to greet you.' He reached for a huge towel and thrust it at her, faint colour flaring over his high cheekbones, his mouth clamped tight over his teeth.

Grabbing at the towel, Lily was suddenly and horribly aware of her nakedness, of the way his brilliant golden eyes had swept her from top to toe and then blanked. Wrapping herself up like a parcel, she watched him shed his wet jacket and walk away, collecting the ring from the vanity on his way back into the bedroom, stepping over her discarded clothing.

Overheated from the prolonged onslaught of hot water and deep embarrassment, Lily plucked up another towel and began to rub her hair dry. In her shock at his abrupt and totally unexpected arrival she'd just stood there, naked as the day she was born, like a transfixed rabbit. Did he think she'd been flaunting herself? Her skin crawled with utter humiliation.

No wonder he'd looked so blank! His preference lay with tall, leggy blondes with all the social graces. He wouldn't want the complication of the bog-standard hired help apparently coming on to him! In his mother's company he would expect her to act like a besotted bride-to-be, but in private he had no interest in her as a woman.

Her face flamed anew when she heard his incisive, 'Wear this. And make it snappy.'

Emerging from the folds of the towel, Lily saw him place a pale amethyst shift dress on the chair that stood just inside the door before he walked back out again. Lacy briefs and matching bra, too—part of the supply that had been bought for her back in London, so that she would look the part he had assigned her: high-maintenance bride-to-be, exactly what his parent would expect to see.

Her tummy squirming, she dressed in the garments he had taken it upon himself to select. Feeling the soft silky fabric of the exquisitely crafted dress touch her skin like a lover's caress made her shudder.

Everything was so wrong. She didn't feel like herself at all. These clothes weren't *her*. In fact, the amount that had been spent on her clothing for a mere fortnight would have kept a family of four for a year, she realised, appalled. Such a waste!'

Her mouth set in mutiny, she stalked into the bedroom, where he was waiting in unconcealed impatience, and announced, 'In future *I* choose what I wear. You might have paid for the stuff—and paid me to lie for you—but you don't own me!'

He shot her a look of exasperation. He was landed with an aggravating, argumentative pest with a body to set male pulses racing. Clueless, too. Left to her own devices she would smother those delectable curves in ugly swamping garments. She should be grateful at being given the sort of beautiful clothes that did credit to her hitherto hidden loveliness, not come at him shouting the odds.

At the memory of her earlier nakedness—which he had done his level best to blank—he felt unwanted heat crawl over his skin, and his voice was a rough undertone as he commanded, 'Come here.'

He swept a silver-backed hairbrush from the dressing table, and as she stubbornly refused to budge he strode over to her and began to stroke the tangles out of her still damp hair, the lean fingers of one hand firmly beneath her chin to stop her wriggling away.

'In future you may choose what to wear.' Her jawbone was so tenderly delicate, her skin so soft beneath the pads of his fingers, her hair like caramel silk. 'Today I hurried you—' He broke off, aware that he was doing something totally unprecedented, trying to placate an argumentative employee. Oddly, his voice was emerging like soft velvet. Clearing his throat roughly, he continued, 'My mother is so anxious to meet her future daughter-in-law. I can't bear to keep her waiting. I know how long women take to dress and fuss over their appearance.'

At the 'future daughter-in-law' falsehood Lily snapped out of the dizzy, intoxicating trance she'd fallen into the moment he'd touched her, stroked the brush through her hair, his magnificent body so close to hers. Stepping away from him, and drawing herself up to her full insignificant height, horrified by her weakness where he was concerned she reminded him, 'I am *nothing* like your usual vanity-obsessed lady-friends! So don't treat me as if I am!'

'Stop arguing.' Curbing impatience, Paolo slipped the fabulous ring back on her finger. There was a feisty glitter in those big grey eyes. Present her to his parent while she was in this mood and the whole thing would be over before it began. Trust him to pick a woman who couldn't hide her feelings!

He needed a purring kitten, not a spitting cat. There was only one thing to do. His hands going to her slim shoulders, he bent his dark head and kissed her.

CHAPTER FIVE

As HIS beautiful mouth took hers Lily was utterly swamped by the shattering emotion which crashed through her with the force of a hurricane. She had never experienced anything remotely like this before. It blew her mind.

Totally incapable of rational thought, she felt instinct take over, and her lips parted to give him better access to the sweetness within. Her entire body was shuddering helplessly as his arms slid from her shoulders to her tiny waist to hold her more closely, to meld her to his lean, powerful length.

She had been kissed before, but never like this—like fire and honey, every cell in her body singing in uncontrolled response as his tongue slid deeper in sensual exploration. Her mindless caressing fingers revelled in the feel of taut muscles beneath the fine fabric of his shirt, and her hands suddenly gripped his wide shoulders in wild reaction as she felt his hot, hard arousal against the quivering softness of her tummy.

Reduced to an unthinking mass of sensation, she raised her hips to press against him, moving with instinct-driven feverish urgency. She heard him groan as a long shudder raced through him, and when his hands slid down to her buttocks, pressing her even closer, the blood in her veins ignited and fierce desire pulsed insistently through her trembling body.

Lily hadn't known that such sensations could exist. Intoxicated, she slid her hands around his magnificent torso, fingers fumbling at the buttons of his shirt because she couldn't get close enough to him. He felt the same. She knew he did. Because his hands were moving restively over her silk-clad body with hungry heat, and then they were sliding the hem of her dress up around her thighs, and the part of her mind that was still amazingly capable of halfway rational thought registered that he was consumed by the same high-voltage passion that was thrumming through every cell of her body. And it was glorious!

Until with a driven groan Paolo lifted his head and held her away from him.

Struggling to retrieve her breath, shocked into immobility, Lily was held by the unfathomable depths of those shimmering golden eyes, partly screened by thickly dark lashes. She could drown in those eyes, she thought shakily, dazed, her tingling, sensitised body still in recovery from the emotional onslaught of his raw passion.

'We should go,' Paolo reminded her in a low, thickened murmur. His hand, not quite steady, reached out for hers, his eyes drawn to her enticing, incredibly responsive body, to her gleaming eyes and flushed cheeks.

He wasn't at all sure what had happened. He felt heat crawl over his skin and his driven admission, 'That was amazing,' pole-axed him—because he hadn't consciously meant to confide that opinion. He didn't know where it had come from. It had simply happened—as if they shared a bond, a passion that went soul-deep.

He pulled in a deep, ragged breath. Before this moment his comments had never, ever been unguarded, and he had always mildly despised those who spoke without thinking through the consequences of what they said.

Fortunately he had the belated good sense to put the shutters up and not voice his further opinion that if his frail parent hadn't been eagerly waiting for them their kiss would have ended up far, far differently. On that bed. And that would have been a disaster. He lived by his own set of rules, and one of them stated that female employees, no matter how attractive, were off-limits.

As it was, though, he had achieved his initial objective, he tried to console himself. Lily Frome looked the image of the blushing bride-to-be. Soft and pink, about to melt into his arms at the first opportunity. But that didn't give him the satisfaction he had thought it would, he recognised uneasily.

Thankfully, the walk down to the small salon on the ground floor gave him time to get his libido back under strict control. What had happened, he rationalised, had been due to base lust. He hadn't been with a woman for a long while, and seeing Lily Frome in all her delicate, promising nakedness had acted on his male libido like a flame on petrol.

Given the circumstances, his initial decision to kiss her, nothing more, had been logical—a means to an end. The outcome, the loss of control on his part—and on hers?—was regrettable. But entirely normal given his months of celibacy.

Thankfully his voice emerged sounding reassuringly normal, too, as he paused before an ornately carved fruitwood door and advised, 'Just be yourself and you will delight her.'

Lily at last came down to earth with a bump, her befuddled mind clearing at the speed of light. Was he being sarcastic? Of course he was—what else? 'Being herself' meant being a dead ordinary, nose-to-the-grindstone, unsophisticated simple girl. In short, the type of woman he wouldn't give a second glance. He knew that.

And yet... Memories of that kiss slammed back to scorch her brain. Vividly recalling the greedy way she'd responded, she blushed furiously and knew she was about to sink into a morass of super-heated suffocating shame.

But it hadn't been all one-way traffic, she told herself defensively.

He had kissed her as if he'd meant it. Passionately. She'd had little or no time for boyfriends in her busy life, but she wasn't stupid. She knew when a man was aroused. And he had been. So that had to mean he had wanted more than kisses.

Heat engulfed her entire body and her breathing shortened. She was horribly aware that he was now looking at her with shimmering, assessing eyes, and she hunched her shoulders, hoping the cringing posture would disguise the shameful way her breasts were peaking and tingling beneath the silk.

'Hold your head up,' he uttered scathingly, irked by the way she was looking—like a woman about to face a firing squad rather than the glowing bride-to-be of a few minutes earlier. Then, remembering he had to tread softly around her, he advised more gently, 'No one's going to eat you, *cara*! Leave most of the talking to me. And remember I'll be right beside you—holding your hand!'

That was meant to reassure her? Hollowly, Lily decided it didn't. Being around him always made her uneasy. Vulnerable. Far too aware of his dynamic sexual appeal. And now, after what had happened, she was fearfully aware of how easily he could cut through her flimsy resistance. Panic skittered through each and every nerve-ending.

She wasn't simple-minded. She knew he didn't even like her. She irritated him. Normally he wouldn't dream of coming on to her; she would be beneath his lofty notice. But, walking in on her nakedness, he had decided, Hey, she'd been bought and paid for, so why not enjoy the action for a couple of weeks? The trouble was, what had happened back in her room told her that she would probably do nothing to discourage him. She shuddered helplessly, hating what she'd discovered about herself.

Opening the door, Paolo dropped her hand and slid his arm around her waist, drawing her with him over the threshold into an elegant room, with white walls, white drapes, cream upholstery and crystal bowls of scented hothouse flowers on every available surface.

Seeing the frail white-haired lady seated at a circular table in the deep window embrasure, Lily felt her heart twist in her breast. She dragged in a deep breath and wished she could disappear in a puff of smoke. The situation was growing more scary with every moment that passed, and she felt truly dreadful over the part she was expected to play.

The radiance of Signora Venini's welcoming smile made her feel even worse, but as if he sensed it Paolo gave her waist a reassuring squeeze and strode forward, bent to give his parent a gentle hug and drop a kiss on the fragile skin of her pale cheek. 'Mamma, I'm so sorry you've been kept waiting. My fault entirely. When I'm with Lily I forget how time flies.'

He had dropped the more formal 'Madre', and Lily could scarcely believe the change in him. His voice so tender, his smile so gentle, his respect very obvious. Nothing like the man she had come to know: austerely impatient, critical, and often cold—a man who bowed to no one.

He obviously adored his mother and cared deeply for her. Against all her principles Lily could reluctantly understand where he was coming from. And sympathise. Or almost.

She still didn't think lying was right, but Paolo truly believed it best to pretend that his future with the woman of his choice was settled, in order to put his fragile mother's mind at ease.

Her heart was pattering against her ribs as the elderly lady extended a slim white hand. Her smile was warm but her voice was feeble as she said, 'Lily—how lovely to meet you at last. Come, sit with me. Paolo has told me so much about you.'

Paolo smiled his encouragement but Lily could see the strain behind it, and, despite her distaste for deceiving the fragile woman, it gave her the necessary impetus to move forward, sit on one of the vacant chairs around the table, smile and lie her socks off. 'And I'm happy to meet you, too,' she greeted her, because Paolo, now stationed directly behind her, his hands on her shoulders, was clearly desperately anxious for his surviving parent, and up close Lily could see why.

Signora Venini looked as if the slightest breeze would disintegrate her frail body. More than the recent scar that ran beneath the line of her snowy white hair—that would heal and eventually disappear—it was the lines of utter weariness, of sadness, etched on her once beautiful features that told a story of a woman who had been tired of living for a long while.

Lily's tender heart felt wrung out as she unconsciously covered the opulent family betrothal ring with the fingers of her other hand and blurted sincerely, the words tumbling out, 'You've been through a major operation, *signora*. You need plenty of rest, peace and quiet—not visitors!' And, despite the warning tightening of Paolo's fingers on her shoulders, she ploughed on, verbalising as much of the truth as she dared because she needed to be out of here. Needed to put as much distance between her and the man she now knew could make her act like a sex-starved trollop as soon as possible.

'I told Paolo that under the circumstances I didn't think the timing of this visit was at all sensible. It could easily have waited until you were feeling stronger.' She managed a smile which she hoped would come over as conspiratorial. 'But you will know how stubborn Paolo can be! Even so, I think it would be best if I left tomorrow, or the day after at the latest, and didn't intrude further on your recuperation period.'

Lily smiled softly, willing the older woman to agree, but her slim hopes were crushed when she got a decidedly firm, 'Nonsense! Getting to know my son's future wife will be the best tonic I could possibly have! The one bright spot in a year that has been so awful!'

Amazingly, the older woman's tawny eyes sparked now with lively determination. 'And for us to get to know each other time is needed, *si*? In fact I expect my son to persuade you to stay with us for much longer than the mere two weeks he promised me—we have a wedding to arrange!'

* * *

'You've got to put a stop to this!' Lily hissed frantically half an hour later when Carla, Paolo's mother's friendly but firm companion, appeared to chivvy the reluctant older woman away for a rest before dinner.

'Silenzio!' An inescapable hand shot out to take her wrist. 'Keep your voice down,' he ordered in the same driven undertone. 'You will be heard. Come.'

Her legs feeling like jelly, her heart pounding fit to suffocate her, Lily was led by one very determined male out of the room, across the marble-slabbed hall, down two corridors and out of a side door to a massive paved terrace, with loungers set to catch the evening sunlight at one side and a long teak table and benches set beneath a vine-covered arbour at the other.

Ignoring the choice of seating, Paolo led her down a shallow flight of stone steps to the garden—a maze of box-bordered paths, sentinel cypress trees and an abundance of roses in leaf and promising bud.

Only when she tripped did he slow his pace, an arm going round her to steady her. 'We sit. And we talk with sense.'

Registering from that slight slip in his usually impeccable English that he was almost as disturbed as she by the afternoon's events, Lily sat—was glad to—as he brought her to a carved marble bench seat beside an antique stone fountain.

Confident that he would be as horrified as she by his mother's excited wedding plans, she started, 'There has to be a way to put her off! You got us into this mess—

now get us out of it! I did my best—told her I had a charity to run and couldn't commit to anything else for ages. But she didn't listen!'

'Total waste of breath,' he incised without hesitation. 'Mamma knows I've stepped in. When I become involved things happen and happen smoothly. That being so, she would know that *because* everything is in hand your absence would be of little or no consequence,' he insulted blandly.

Fit to spit bricks, Lily glared at him. Arrogant brute! 'Then put your so-superior brain in gear and think of something!'

Anger lit her big grey eyes. But something else sparked within those luminous depths. Fright?

Settling beside her, Paolo draped an arm along the back of the seat. Deliberately relaxing his body. Two of them indulging in hysterics would get them precisely nowhere.

'I admit I didn't expect her to launch straight into immediate wedding plans with such gusto,' he confessed, his lips curving in appreciation of the stony glare she gave him—until her scathing response set a slow burn of discomfited heat running over his cheekbones.

'No, you expected her to be gasping her last and whispering about how happy she was, going to her maker knowing that you were settling down to marriage!'

The moment the words were out Lily regretted them—hated herself for even thinking them, never mind flinging them at him.

Her soft heart ruling her head, she offered softly,

'I'm sorry. That was a horrible thing to say.' She reached for his hand, clenched on his knee, and curled slim fingers around it. 'Of course you've been worried about your mum. When someone we love is ill we can't help it—can't help dwelling on the worst-case scenario, praying it won't happen but desperately afraid it will. It's quite natural.'

His hand was still a fist beneath her cool fingers. Affronted dignity was written on his stunning features. Mindful that she was probably irritating the hell out of him, she added uncertainly, 'I wish I had a mum to worry about.'

Paolo's shuttered eyes switched to find hers. Warmth curled around his heart, squeezed it. Lily Frome. Those huge eyes were drenched with the softness of sympathy, lush lips quivering slightly. In spite of her diminutive size she had a big heart, was so unused to hurting anyone she was swift to apologise when she felt she had.

And he had variously bullied, insulted and ridden roughshod over her. She didn't deserve that. He had kissed her, and yet he knew next to nothing about her. That was an insult in itself.

Uncurling his fist, he laced his fingers between hers. 'What happened to her?'

Taken aback, Lily blinked. Her soft mouth parted, then clamped shut again. Something really weird happened to her when he was being nice to her. She tried to analyse it and couldn't.

He prompted gently, 'Well?'

'I—' Lily was floundering. It was the look in his eyes that did it. The golden gleam was assessing, yet kind, warm. His hard male mouth had softened. As if she were a human being with feelings instead of an employee paid to do as she was told—an automaton that he could switch on and then switch off and put back in the cupboard and forget about when the task was completed to his satisfaction. It was unnerving.

'She died,' she got out. 'When I was a baby. I don't remember her.' She smiled shakily, her eyes meeting his at last. 'I do have a few photographs, though. She was really pretty.'

'Then you must take after her.' His fingers tightened on hers. 'And your father?'

He thought she was pretty? She sucked her lower lip between her teeth. His hand, laced with hers, felt so good. Too good. She wished it didn't. Wished she had the strength of mind to snatch her hand away. But she hadn't.

Lily lifted her slender shoulders in a tiny shrug. 'He left. He handed me over to my mother's aunt. There were no other relatives.'

'How often do you see him? Hear from him?'

Her chin lifted at his suddenly grim tone. 'Never. OK? Though, to be fair to him, my parents married young. Too young. They were still in their teens when I was born. I guess he couldn't cope with the demands of a baby. I must have been a mistake. I expect he thought he and Mum would have years of married life together before they had to settle down to be parents.

He would have seen letting Great-Aunt Edith adopt me as the best thing for me.'

Dio! Paolo's eyes widened in perplexity. How could a man hand over a tiny scrap of his own flesh and blood and walk away? Yet she was making excuses for the inexcusable! Did she always turn the other cheek? Look for the good where others could see only bad? If so, she was unique in his experience!

He was looking at her as if she were from another planet, Lily registered, confused. She moistened her dry lips, parted them to stress that her lack of parents had nothing to do with the knotty problem they were facing, then promptly forgot what she'd been about to tell him when he leaned forward, sliding his arms around her as he kissed her.

Tender this time. Achingly tender. Amazingly beautiful. And her head was spinning, her heart hurting, when he broke the kiss, held her head into his shoulder and murmured softly, 'I've given you a hard time. It is my turn to apologize, *cara*. It won't happen again.'

Where had that come from? Never apologise, never explain—what had happened to the code he lived by?

Shaken with the depth of what he was feeling—compassion, admiration, disgust with his earlier unfeeling treatment of her, whatever—he turned his head to touch his lips to the so-vulnerable spot below her ear.

'Trust me. I got us into this mess, just as you said, and I'll get us out of it.' He could feel her heart beating beneath her perfect breasts. Nameless emotion claimed him and his voice was dark and husky as he told her, 'In the meantime relax, enjoy being here.'

He almost added *with me*, but stopped himself in time.

CHAPTER SIX

SHE was becoming addicted to him, Lily admitted with agitation. Really addicted to him. When he was with her, by her side, in the same room, meeting up with his mother for lunch or dinner, she couldn't take her eyes off him, and when he turned his beautifully shaped head, caught her moony eyes on him and gave her that lazy, sexy smile of his, she just about went to pieces.

Did he know that? Know that he only had to smile at her, casually touch her hand in passing, rest his hand lightly on her shoulder, to make her breathing quicken, her heart leap, her body sting and burn with sexual tension?

She had the terrifying feeling that she was falling in love with him, and she so didn't want to! Why, in full knowledge of what she was looking at, would she want to buy a one-way ticket to a place called Misery?

She could tell herself with cold, stark truth that this new display of tender togetherness he'd displayed during the couple of days they'd been here was just an act, but it didn't make the slightest bit of difference.

And as for kissing her—well, she'd worked that out too. Without any trouble whatsoever. Both times he kissed her had been when she'd displayed serious misgivings or signs of mutiny. In that first instance, her deep reluctance to meet his mother, and in the second her hysterics over his mother's insistence on making plans for a wedding that wasn't going to happen.

He was manipulating her, but knowing that didn't make a scrap of difference either. And that made her the worst kind of fool—her own worst enemy.

Her cheeks pink with annoyance—at herself, mostly—she swiftly tucked her shirt into the waistband of the classic cream-coloured linen skirt she'd selected from the abundance of fabulous garments Donatella had unpacked for her, ran a comb through her gleaming jaw-length fall of hair, and added just a touch of gloss to her lips. Looking in the mirror, she smiled wryly at the understated high-maintenance reflection she saw there, and set off to obey Carla's summons, issued from the house phone near her bedside five minutes earlier.

Signora Venini was taking her morning airing on the terrace and would be pleased if Signorina Lily would join her.

It would be the first time she'd been alone with Paolo's mother, and the prospect made her feel even more nervous. Without his presence as a buffer who knew what she might let slip by unguarded word or look? Especially if the older woman brought up the scream-inducing subject of wedding arrangements. She just wasn't used to pretending to be what she wasn't. Living a lie.

Paolo, as he'd informed her last night, would be spending most of the day in Florence on business. He'd invited her to go with him—to hit the shops, do the tourist thing until he was ready to return. She'd refused flatly, wanting time alone to get her head straight, talk herself out of what she was beginning to feel for him, put in some hard work on her sense of self-preservation.

Now she wished she'd accepted his invitation, if only to avoid the coming *tête-à-tête* and the pitfalls it was sure to present.

Reaching the doors to the terrace, Lily allowed herself a moment to let the soft light and gentle warmth of the Tuscan spring wash over her, and hopefully begin to relax her, starting slightly when a cheerful, '*Buongiorno*, Lily!' hit her ears.

'*Signora*,' Lily responded feebly, her feet carrying her with a reluctance she hoped didn't show towards the table beneath the vine-covered loggia, where the old lady sat in the dappled shade.

'Sit with me. And do you think you could manage to call me Fiora? Less formal, *si*?' Her smile was pure charm. Lily now knew where Paolo had got it from. When it suited him! '"Mamma" we will save until the happy day when you are my daughter-in-law.'

Knowing that day would never dawn, Lily felt slightly sick as she forced herself forward and sank into a chair on the opposite side of the table.

How she hated deceiving this nice old lady! Part of her was strongly urging her to come clean, confess all, put her conscience to rest and weather the storm that would erupt from Paolo's direction. But then Fiora said, 'How pretty you look—my cynical son has followed his heart and at last chosen well. A lovely young thing in possession of a loving and gentle heart, instead of a glossy model with a calculating machine where her heart should be! You are going to make him very happy!'

All Lily could manage was a painted on smile that covered the sinking conviction that there was no way she could tell Paolo's mother the truth—because not only would it shatter the old lady's obvious happiness, it would cause a deep rift between mother and son, and she couldn't bring herself to be responsible for that.

Thankfully, Agata arrived with a tray of coffee, and while Fiora was pouring from the elegant silver pot she confided, 'The nurse my son hired has departed—such a bossy creature! I told Paolo that as I felt so much better she was not needed.'

'And he agreed?' He was so protective of his mother, so anxious for her well-being, that Lily couldn't keep the note of sheer astonishment out of her voice.

'Not without argument!' The hazel eyes lit with laughter, and Lily reflected that Paolo's mother did look better. There was colour in her cheeks and strength in her voice now, and the faint bruising around her eyes had disappeared. 'He had to agree that the news of his wedding has given me a new lease of life!' She reached out a hand to cover Lily's, where it lay on the sun-warmed wood of the tabletop, and confided soberly, 'My husband's death ten years ago was a terrible blow. Sergio and I were very dear to each other. But I had my two handsome sons to live for. The hope of grandchildren.'

She sighed, withdrew her hand and laid it with the other in her lavender silk lap. 'Then, just over a year ago, my son Antonio and his pregnant wife died in a car accident. Another dreadful blow. And Paolo, to my sorrow, seemed quite determined never to marry again.' She shrugged her thin shoulders. 'In a way I could understand his reluctance. He couldn't trust his emotions, you see. Twice they'd let him down very badly. But of course he will have told you all this.'

With effort, Lily nodded, cringing inside. Another lie! Paolo wouldn't confide in her, tell her anything personal. She was a mere employee, fit for carrying out his orders and nothing more. She could tell Fiora that it hadn't been his emotions that had let him down because he didn't have any—not real ones—except in respect of his adored mother. It was all down to a low boredom threshold, as Penny Fleming had explained. But she'd hold her tongue and let the old lady keep her fond illusions.

'Apart from a mother's natural wish to see her son happy and settled, I knew that if Paolo didn't marry the ancient bloodline my Sergio was rightly so proud of would die out, and that was another great sadness to me. But—' a smile broke through the miasma of sad memories '—he has found you, lost his heart and found a happy future. So, after a long and painful year I can look forward to the future with a sense of joy I had never expected to know again.'

It was the first Lily had heard of the tragedy, and Fiora's year of hopeless depression. At last she could fully understand why Paolo, on hearing of his mother's possibly fatal illness, had decided to lie. He would have been at his wits' end, and must have seen announcing a fake engagement as the only way to give his adored mother a measure of happiness.

But fully empathising with him now didn't make the deception any easier. It made it harder.

She was relieved when Fiora's companion appeared, to chivvy the older woman into taking her morning rest.

'To get your strength back you must rest often,' Carla stated with a sideways smile for Lily, holding out a hand to help the older woman to her feet.

'Lily and I were having an important conversation,' Fiora objected with hauteur, waving aside the proffered hand. 'And I can walk unaided! Leave us—I am not in the least tired.'

'That is because you have behaved sensibly up to now and rested, as your consultant said you should,' Carla countered levelly, and Lily hid a smile, wondering who would win this contest of wills. Her money was on Fiora!

She would have lost it, she recognised sickly, when Carla delivered the power punch. 'You will need all your strength to plan for and attend the wedding you're so excited about. Tire yourself and you will be fit for nothing!'

Fiora rose to her feet promptly at that remark, admitting, 'For once you are quite right.' The smile she gave Lily was pure mischief. 'I will see you and Paolo at dinner this evening. I have something exciting to tell you both.' And she allowed herself to be led away, grumbling, 'Remember, Carla, that if you get to be too bossy you will go the way of the nurse!'

Her companion's comfortable grin showed she knew the threat was hot air and bluster and certainly not meant.

As soon as the other two had entered the imposing villa Lily leapt to her feet, too wired to sit still one moment longer. Why was Paolo absent when she really needed him?

Her hands clenched into fists at her sides, she paced over to the stone balustrade and stared unseeingly out at the view over thickly wooded hillsides and fertile valleys. In her opinion Paolo was far too laid-back about the situation he had catapulted them into.

She had to make him understand that he must somehow put an end to talk of imminent wedding bells! *Now.* Right now! Before they found themselves even deeper enmeshed in Fiora's plans!

She had tried on the occasion of her first meeting with his mother. Stressing her need to be home, working, because it was all hands on deck as far as the charity went.

To no avail.

So it was up to him. And since he wasn't around, and she felt she'd go stir-crazy if she thought about it for one more moment, she'd have to do something to take her mind off it.

Turning on the heels of her supple leather courts, she headed smartly for the villa, slipping up to her room, settling on the side of the bed and picking up the phone. The nerve-racking situation made her feel as if she was fighting her way through dense clouds, no map to give her directions, and the best person to help her feel grounded again was her great-aunt.

Edith picked up on the second ring, her customary no-nonsense, 'Yes, who is this?' bringing the first real smile to Lily's lips for days.

'Me, Aunt. How are you coping alone?' Suddenly she could see a possible way out. 'Short-handed, it must be difficult. Did you find someone to exercise Maisie's dog?' If she could get her great-aunt to admit that in her absence the charity couldn't meet its obligations she'd have the perfect excuse to cut her stay in Italy short.

'Don't fuss, child! We are coping beautifully. Kate Johnson is in place. She came early. And as soon as she'd settled into her accommodation at Felton Hall she started to organise the volunteers. She's found two—got the vicar to plead for help after his sermon—and is advertising for more in the local paper. She even managed to get Life Begins a good write-up. I can't think why we didn't think to do that ourselves! It takes a well-paid professional to get things right. Even at this early stage everything is looking far more hopeful. I would have thought that young man of yours would have told you all this. He's in daily touch by telephone. He's obviously taking his involvement very seriously.'

'Young man of yours'? She couldn't mean Paolo, could she? How absurd? Lily fell into a glum silence, her escape route well and truly blocked. She was glad for the charity's sake, of course she was, but it didn't help her situation. Which, she admitted uncomfortably, was really selfish of her.

'You still there?' The volume of the question made Lily flinch and squawk an affirmative, holding the receiver away from her ear as her great-aunt boomed on, 'So no need to fuss! Now, are you having a lovely time?' Thankfully not waiting for an answer, she continued, 'When our new partner suggested he give you a holiday in Italy, mentioning that his mother had recently been ill and could do with some young company, and that you looked very tired, I realised I had been neglecting your welfare. You've been working far too hard for too long…'

Lily mentally shut out the unnecessarily loud one-sided conversation. So *that* was how he had persuaded Edith to agree, without questioning his motives, to allow her to go to Italy without any fuss. She had often wondered. But she should have known he could charm the birds out of the trees when he had to. When Paolo Venini wanted something he got it. One way or another.

Cutting into a pause for breath at the other end of

the line, she said, 'Look after yourself, Aunt. And I'll see you soon.'

At least she devoutly hoped so.

Paolo swung the car onto the long curving drive up to the villa. He was running late. He would be hard-pressed to shower and change before dinner, taken at the earlier hour of seven as a concession to his mother's recuperation. His meetings had run on for longer than he'd expected, and for some reason he'd been anxious to get home, so he hadn't been his usual incisive self. His mind had been elsewhere.

Because he wanted to see Lily? Be with her? The thought flickered briefly, unwelcomely, across his mind. Of course not! Or if he did then it would only be to check things out, reassure himself that she hadn't, without his presence, his guidance, done or said something to give the game away.

His strong jaw tightened. He gave thanks hourly for his mother's recovery. That it had been hugely helped along by his fictitious engagement gave him pause. But he hadn't expected her to jump on the wedding band wagon with such spritely agility! Only yesterday she had been pestering him to seek an appointment with the priest, fix a date for as soon as possible after her final appointment with her surgeon.

When he told her, as he would have to, that there was to be a lengthy postponement she would be disappointed. He knew that. But she would understand the importance of a sudden—invented—crisis. A need for him to travel to his headquarters in New York, Madrid, London or wherever. His need to clear business before he could settle down to married life. She had been married to the head of a world-renowned mercantile bank for long enough to know that the sound running of the business came before personal considerations. Another bending of the truth. Distasteful but necessary.

Removing Lily, whom she had confessed happily that she'd taken to her heart, would pose a different problem. The excuse that she was needed back in England to work with the charity wouldn't wash because his mother knew he had intervened and thus made Lily redundant.

But he had the problem solved. Her great-aunt was elderly. Needed her. His mother would understand that—understand that depriving an old lady of the company and care of the great-niece she had adopted as a small baby, loved as if she were her own child, would be unkind. Thus, the engagement would stretch and stretch, until some time in the future he could say that long engagements didn't work and the wedding was off.

Hopefully by that time his mother would be much stronger, more able to handle the disappointment. There would be recriminations coming his way, but his shoulders were broad. That his thinking was devious, to put it mildly, was in no way a pleasure to him. Normally direct, he found deceit left a bad taste in his mouth. But in this case the ends—his beloved mother's return to good health—justified the means.

He would have to explain all this to Lily. His jaw relaxed. Put her out of her misery! Though, to do her credit, she had acted the part he'd assigned her more convincingly than he'd expected.

Her role as a woman who was deeply in love couldn't be faulted. Nothing personal—she knew the financial viability of her charity depended on her co-operation—but the way she looked at him, her eyes dreamy, her cheeks flushing with pleasure when he smiled at her, silver lights sparkling in the clear depths of her eyes was completely convincing. And when he touched her, took her hand, slipped an arm around her tiny waist to draw her forward to join the conversation between himself and Mamma, he would hear the catch of her breath, watch as the pulse-beat at the base of her slender neck quickened and see those lush lips part. He was hard put to see a flaw in her performance. She had a totally unexpected acting ability.

Such kissable lips, too, as he'd discovered. Had her response been play-acting, too? Somehow he didn't think so. Unconsciously, a softly sensual smile curved his long mouth. Who would have believed that the muddy scrap of his initial acquaintance could have been transformed into such a delicate, bewitching beauty?

Sexily responsive, too. Heat rolled through him and his body surged at the memory, and, unbidden, the aching need to hold her again, take that generous mouth, and take things further, much further, gripped him with driven savagery.

Basta! Enough! Braking the powerful car in a shower of gravel, he exited, shutting the door with enough force to shatter the silence. Having sex with Lily Frome, no matter how irritatingly tempting the prospect seemed, was a road he was *not* going to travel! Quite apart from the fact that she was temporarily his employee, and therefore strictly out of bounds, she was not his type.

His type. A heavy frown scored his forehead. Tall, blonde, leggy, polished. He'd been briefly engaged to one and almost as briefly married to another. That was before he'd learned the hard way that commitment was for fools. And now the blondes—when he could be bothered—were still tall, eye-worthy, polished and clued-up, taking a casual, sophisticated affair in their leggy stride. Cool, knowing the rules of the game.

Ergo, Lily Frome was *not* his type! She was tiny. But perfectly formed. She had hair the colour of a toffee apple. She was sweet, caring, not afraid to answer back, open and honest, so disturbed by what he had as good as coerced her into doing that she probably had nightmares every time she went to bed.

Went to bed— He strode into the villa by a side door, slipped up to the first storey by the staff staircase, to avoid meeting anyone, and tried to push the connection between Lily and bed right out of his mind. Mention a casual affair to her and she'd run a mile. Screaming!

Or hit him with the nearest heavy object!

And he, for one, wouldn't blame her. She was gorgeous, warm-hearted, intrinsically good, and she deserved far, far better than that. She deserved someone who would love her, value and treasure her.

Lily knew she was running around like a headless chicken. A naked headless chicken!

She'd put off having a shower and changing for dinner in the hope of waylaying Paolo on his return. Because she'd known she would explode if she didn't corner him and make him do something about his poor deluded mother and her talk of weddings!

But half an hour before the appointed time for the formal dinner *en famille* that Fiora enjoyed so much he still hadn't arrived. Giving up hope, she'd sprinted into the shower and out again in record time, then scuttled around, pulling on fresh underwear, plucking something in a lovely smoky blue colour out of the wardrobe and dragging it on—only to find that though the front of the dress was modest enough it left most of her back bare down to her waist, leaving her bra straps exposed. And the skirt was as bad—it sort of clipped her bottom before flaring down to her ankles, showing a glaringly obvious panty line.

Muttering something that would have had her great-aunt telling her to wash her mouth out with soap and water, she stripped off to her skin, started to pull the dress on again, then threw it onto the bed, diving for the well-stocked cupboard and throwing garments out, looking for something that wouldn't show all her underwear.

* * *

'Lily…' The words that would have had him asking how her day had gone flew out of his head. If there'd been problems then suddenly they weren't important. He'd walked into her room unannounced, as if he had the right. To find her naked, flushed. Bewildered?

His breath caught. A hard tight knot in his chest. He should apologise, retreat.

He found himself moving forward instead, closing the door behind him. Tugged towards her as if he had no will of his own. She was exquisite. A surge of sexual need swamped him. He stopped breathing.

She should be backing away. Angry. But she wasn't.

Her tiny bare feet seemed rooted to the carpet. Did she feel, as he did, that this was meant? Fated? That there was nothing either of them could do about it? Always in charge of his own destiny, this was a first for him.

Closer. His eyes found hers and held. Her clear wide gaze made his heart turn over. Her soft lips were parted in unconscious invitation. The delicate pink crests of her perfect creamy breasts peaked in betrayal. Did she burn for him as he burned for her?

One touch of his hand, his unsteady hand, his skin against her skin and there would be no turning back. As he knew his own name he knew that. Her slender body was a siren call. Irresistible.

He dragged a breath into his oxygen-starved lungs. Lily was an innocent. Not his type, not the usual blonde sophisticate who saw good sex as a fair exchange for a few weeks of his attention, fancy restaurants, weekends in Paris, St Tropez, Rome, taking a parting gift of some costly jewel or other with no regrets.

The feeling that he would die before harming Lily, hurting her, overwhelmed him.

Turning, he reached for the control he'd almost lost during the handful of minutes that had passed since he'd walked in on her, reached for a robe flung carelessly over the back of a chair and enclosed her in it as she looked up at him in a way that turned his insides to water.

The backs of his fingers drifted over the warm skin that covered her delicate collarbone as he closed the fabric, and it was almost his undoing. His voice was thicker, more brusque than he'd intended, as he stepped away, putting much needed distance between them, and gave his belated apology, 'Forgive me. Walking in without your invitation to enter was crass.' He gave a cursory glance at his wristwatch. 'Dinner in five minutes. Mamma will be waiting.' And he left before he could succumb to the heartbreaking confusion in her beautiful eyes.

CHAPTER SEVEN

'I HAVE a lovely surprise for you!'

Fiora had waited until the sea bass had been served by the now silently departing Donatella, and Lily noted with a sinking feeling that her eyes were sparking with excitement.

'We are to have an engagement party on Friday!' she announced. 'The first social gathering we have hosted in over a year! This afternoon I have arranged everything on the telephone.'

'Have you, now?' Carla, exotic in a deep scarlet flowing gown that suited her ample figure, patrician features and glossy black hair put in repressively. 'While my back was turned?'

'Exactly.'

'And you don't think you should have waited until you are strong enough to cope with such excitement and busyness?'

'Mamma?' Paolo echoed the companion's question, and for the first time since entering the dining room Lily looked directly at him, willing him to veto his mother's insane idea.

In his white dinner jacket he looked exactly what he was—sophisticated, urbane, perfectly at home in his exquisite surroundings. White on white. White walls, long windows where gauzy white drapes fluttered, tall white candles on the table drawing gleaming reflections from the antique silverware, Venetian glass and sparkling china. White blooms in a creamy porcelain bowl gracing the centre of the table.

Lily's lashes swiftly screened her tortured eyes. Watching him idly toy with the stem of his wine glass, relaxed, his sensual mouth softening even as he raised one strongly marked eyebrow in the direction of his mother, she felt as if someone had kicked her in the stomach.

She didn't think she would ever, ever be able to face him alone again! A raging blush burned her face. The way she'd just stood there, for the second time caught as naked as a newborn, stunned, immobile, watching the slow drift of his golden eyes as he moved towards her, trapped by a fierce sexual tension. It must have seemed to him that she was blatantly inviting him to touch her, make love to her!

Which was exactly what she had been doing, she recognised with searingly painful honesty. She had wanted him so very desperately that her normal sense of modesty and self-respect had departed without a single trace!

But he couldn't have made his lack of interest any

plainer. Apologising for his intrusion and covering her up with that robe. And leaving. A definite *thanks, but no thanks*! She had never felt so humiliated, so deeply ashamed of herself in her life!

It had taken more courage than she had imagined she possessed to pull on the most sober garment she could find and appear for dinner. Now, she belatedly wished she had taken the coward's way out—pleaded a headache and buried herself deep beneath the bedclothes, refusing to come out until this nightmare had gone away.

'Don't fuss, Paolo!' Fiora forked a little of the delicious fish. 'It is to be a small affair only—to mark your betrothal, as is proper. Just your cousins—I know you have no time for them, but I want to show Lily off to what little remains of our family.' She laid down her cutlery after clearing her plate, welcome evidence of her returning appetite. 'As for the extra work—what are staff for? It will give me great pleasure to sit back and simply direct operations!'

Once again Lily steeled herself to raise her eyes in Paolo's direction, swallowing shakily as the impact of his lean male beauty hit her. Tightening her soft pink mouth as her heart clattered against her ribs, she waited for him to put a halt to it all—rule out any idea of an engagement party. After all, he was king of the roost. This was his home, his fake engagement.

But all he said was, 'Then, provided you don't overtire yourself, we will humour you, Mamma.'

Paolo heard Lily's rush of indrawn breath, saw her

slender white shoulders—revealed by the black silk slip dress she was wearing—stiffen, before they sagged as she slipped a little lower in her chair, as if she were trying to hide herself under the table.

Poor sweet Lily! An iron band tightened around his heart. He'd put her through one ordeal after another. He would make amends, he vowed silently. He would make things right if it was the last thing he did.

She had looked strained and subdued since she'd joined them. Because of what had happened—almost happened—back in her bedroom?

His body hardened intolerably as mental images flooded his brain.

He felt he had shown quite remarkable restraint in the circumstances. He had been driven wild by need, yet he had done the honourable thing and backed off. Surely she would understand that by doing that and not following his primal instincts it showed he had grown to respect her, admire her and care for her? That he had put her physical and emotional well-being before his own desire to possess her enticingly sexy body?

When she understood that he had respected her innocence, not taken advantage of what she had undoubtedly unknowingly offered, she would begin to respect him too. Would grow to like him and forget how he had manipulated her into a situation he knew she felt deeply uncomfortable about. For some reason it was vitally important.

What was it about Lily Frome that brought out the male protective instinct in him? The need to look good in her eyes? Until now he had never cared how other people saw him.

His brooding golden gaze rested on her, and his heart squeezed painfully inside his chest. That dress made her look so fragile, threw the pallor of her skin into prominence. She looked achingly delicate. Fragile and breakable.

He didn't want to break her. He wanted to—

Muttering his excuses, he left the table and went to take a long cold shower.

'Lily said she wanted some fresh air,' Fiora said in answer to Paolo's question, not raising her eyes from the lists she was writing, rapidly covering the sheets of paper, underlining some items several times, starring or circling others.

To-do, or Have-done lists for the coming party, he guessed, helping himself to a much-needed cup of unsweetened dark coffee from the pot on her breakfast tray.

His night had been passed in deep thought. His body and mind had thrown up a problem. But, as always, having looked at the problem from all possible angles, he had found the answer.

All he had to do was persuade Lily to reach the same conclusion.

Since his ill-fated disaster of a marriage, and before that his farcical engagement, he had cynically distrusted his judgement where women were concerned. He had found, and subsequently taken it as read, that women would bend over backwards in their haste to fall in with his slightest suggestion because of what was in it for them—being seen with one of Europe's most eligible unattached men in all the right places, being pampered for as long as his interest lasted, and finally departing from his life in receipt of a handsome pay-off.

But he wasn't thinking about his usual type here; he was thinking about Lily. And she was so very different. Which was why—

His brow furrowed as Fiora laid aside a sheet of paper, which from where he was standing looked decidedly covered in hieroglyphics, and remarked with a touch of rebuke, 'The dear girl looked pale and strained. I hope you haven't done something to upset her.'

'Of course not.'

The words stung like acid in his mouth. He'd done nothing *but* upset her since he'd as good as blackmailed her into playing a part she found demeaning and distasteful! He shifted his feet uncomfortably. He wasn't used to being in the wrong. He didn't like it.

'Good. Mind you don't.' The glance his mother gave him was admonitory. 'She is a lovely young woman in all respects, and nothing at all like those dreadful painted harpies you kept getting yourself photographed with—much to my despair!'

Paolo stuffed his hands into the pockets of his off-white chinos. 'Don't nag, Mamma.'

'I am your mother. I shall nag if I wish.'

His long mouth twitched. 'The days of the harpies

are over, I assure you.' Had been for quite some time now. He had discovered that casual affairs were not only a bore, they left him deeply unsatisfied.

'I should think so, too! While you're here I would like your permission to ask my dressmaker to attend. Primarily to create Lily's wedding gown, but I'd also like him to run up something for me—the mother of the groom must look her best.'

His golden eyes lit with laughter. She was priceless. Her 'dressmaker' was one of the most talented and internationally sought-after designers in Italy.

'As you wish, Mamma.' He stooped to drop a kiss on her forehead, anxious now to be off and begin to put his plans into operation, but she caught his hand, holding him, her eyes fond, and gazing up at the son who inspired frustration, exasperation, and above all absolute devotion in the maternal heart.

'As you know, I see that surgeon person in three weeks' time. I would like you to arrange the marriage for as soon as possible after that.'

He raised her hand to his lips, serious now, his eyes darkening. 'Only if you have a clean bill of health and the doctor gives you the go-ahead. Not even my desire for the wedding will allow me to let you overtire yourself.'

'I'll waltz through the consultation—you'll see!' Her smile was radiant. 'And waltz at your wedding! Now, run along—go to your fiancée.'

But finding Lily was no longer his most pressing priority. Things were moving at breakneck speed. What had started off as a deception to make what he had genuinely believed to be his mother's last few days happy had turned into something quite different.

Strong white teeth showed in an unrepentant grin as he strode into his study. There were things to arrange before he set about persuading his pretend fiancée to become his real one and agree to be his wife.

Kill two birds with one stone. Assure Mamma's happiness, her peace of mind, her interest in a bright future, give her the prospect of grandchildren, and at the same time assuage his now deeply felt need to care for Lily, protect her, make love to her, make her his own.

The idea of marrying again didn't seem as distasteful as it had done. Lily would be a wife he could trust, honest and straightforward—except when he coerced her into betraying her principles. His mouth tightened.

He knew he wanted her permanently in his life. And what he wanted he always got.

Didn't he?

His mouth set, he lifted the receiver and began, rapid-fire, to punch in numbers.

Feeling light-headed, Lily sat on the herb-strewn grass, drew her legs up, looped her arms around them and dropped her head down onto her knees.

She'd risen early, creeping through the villa like a thief, intent on avoiding Paolo because being anywhere near him with the memory of the way she'd behaved last evening still raw between them was out of the question.

But her conscience had pricked her when she'd met Carla, taking a breakfast tray into Fiora's room. Paolo's mother had shown her nothing but warmth and kindness since her arrival. She was a lovely lady, and would only worry when her absence was discovered—an absence Lily was determined would last for several hours.

So, worrying the elderly lady being the last thing she wanted to do, she'd poked her head around the door in Carla's wake and said, as brightly as she could, 'Fiora, *buongiorno*!' Paolo's mother had been already up and dressed, bright-eyed and bushy-tailed, a huge notepad on her lap. 'As it's such a lovely morning I thought I'd explore the gardens and maybe grab an hour or two of sunbathing.' And she'd headed off as quickly as she could.

The beautiful gardens were extensive, with many secluded areas where she could sit in solitude. And even though she was sure Paolo wouldn't set out to look for her—his abrupt departure from the dining room last night instead of spending the remainder of the evening with her and his mother, as had been his custom, told her that he'd found that bedroom scene deeply distasteful and would want as little to do with her as possible during the remainder of her stay here—she needed to get right away from the villa's immediate environs for the few hours she desperately needed.

And so when she'd found a wooden door in the high stone perimeter wall she'd pushed it open and found herself out on the open hillside, where she'd sunk down on the grass and scrunched up in a bundle of exhausting emotions, knowing she would need far more than a few hours to get her silly self sorted.

She'd fallen in love with Paolo Venini.

She'd done her best to convince herself that what she felt was nothing more serious than a normal female reaction to a powerfully charismatic and sexy male. Lust. Something that would thankfully and quite rapidly fade when she was no longer constantly in his presence, when all the contact with him she had would be his promised regular and long-distance funding of the charity organiser he'd set in place back in England. A case of out of sight, out of mind.

But he would never be out of her mind. That was the stark, unpalatable truth of it. He would always have a place in her heart, and her heart would ache for him. And her body would cringe with shame whenever she remembered how she'd stood before him, naked and needy.

He had turned his back on her and walked away. After pointedly draping a robe around her, demonstrating his uninterest. And why *wouldn't* he walk away? she asked herself brutally. He could grit his teeth and act a part when they were in his mother's company, for the sake of the deception he had instigated, and he might be highly sexed—one only had to look at the succession of busty blonde bimbos who passed through his life—but skinny, unsophisticated nobodies would leave him cold.

She was just someone he'd paid to play a part. Someone he would never have noticed if he hadn't had a brainstorm and decided to manufacture a fiancée to ease his mother's mind, back when it had seemed unlikely she would survive her operation, let alone recover from it. She had to remember that. It would help her recovery from the illness of falling in love. Someone, somewhere had likened it to an illness, hadn't they?

About to get to her feet and walk off some of her pent-up emotions, Lily tensed, her breath solidifying in her lungs, her pulse going haywire.

She sensed his presence even before he spoke, and her mouth ran dry.

'Lily, are you hiding?'

Deny it? Pretend that bedroom scene hadn't happened? Or face it out? A split second to make up her mind.

She lifted her head. Watched the effortlessly graceful way he sank to the ground beside her and mentally cursed his raw sexual magnetism. But she drew on some reserve of courage and gave him the truth, her small features tight. 'Yes. Hiding. I'm embarrassed about what happened before dinner yesterday, OK? And, if you're wondering, I don't normally make no attempt to cover up when a man walks in on me in my birthday suit. Right?'

And, having said her piece, she quickly changed the subject. 'And I'm mad as blazes at you because you didn't put a stop to that engagement party nonsense when I'm sure you could have done!' She saw him smile and turned her head away sharply, biting down on her soft lower lip, because that smile of his was enough to turn the sanest woman into a gibbering wreck.

'And you have much experience of men surprising you in a state of nakedness?' His voice was as rich and dark as chocolate.

Lily's skin quivered. 'No, of course not!' Why didn't he just drop it? Was he cruel enough to be getting a kick out of embarrassing her?

'I thought not. You are truly an innocent.'

He was sitting so close she could feel his purr of amusement. Or was it more like satisfaction?

Either way, it was one more strike against her! He wouldn't rate lack of experience highly, much less fall in love with an 'innocent' as he had named her. That meant she just had to stop living in cloud-cuckoo land, moping and pining and wishing he would catch the same illness she had come down with! He didn't even fall in love with the type of woman he bedded—cool, blonde, sexy and knowing. He just used them, grew bored, and tossed them aside! So what chance would *she* have?

He might laugh at what he would have seen as an attempt to entice him, so it was up to her to show him she had a mind of her own and wasn't to be sidetracked or poked fun at!

'Don't change the subject.'

'And that is?' he asked, with provocative smoothness, stretching out his long muscular legs, angling his body into hers so that she wanted to move away, right away, but couldn't make herself.

Hot colour scorched her cheekbones. What was the matter with her? She craved his nearness like an addict craved a fix. She knew how bad it was for her, but she couldn't make herself get up and put distance between them. She was a hopeless case where he was concerned!

Furious with herself, she grumped at him. 'That awful engagement party your mother's busy organising! You must stop her before even more people get drawn into our shameful lies!'

'Ah, that.' He touched the side of her face with the backs of his fingers, then withdrew his hand and reached into a pocket to produce a small velvet-covered box.

Her skin still burning from his touch, Lily could only stare transfixed as he slid the dazzling ring onto her wedding finger. 'A perfect fit now. I told you I'd get it altered.'

The smugness in his voice fired her to blazing anger. 'I could slap you!' she hissed, scrambling round so that she was on her knees, facing him. 'I *told* you not to mess with the family heirloom when it's only going to be a stage prop—you stupid, arrogant—'

'My refreshing Lily!' Almost lazily he reached forward, hands on her shoulders, pulling her down to his level, one of his legs pinioning hers. 'You are the first woman to remind me that I am not perfect! The only woman apart from Mamma who has the spirit to argue with me—I like that.' He dropped the lightest of kisses onto the end of her nose. 'I like it very much. It reminds me that I am human.'

His nearness, the heat of his body against hers, the scent of his skin, were desperately tantalising, and made her tremble. She loved him so much, and she hated herself for loving him. She just knew that her resolve to keep him firmly at arm's length was rapidly dwindling, like mist in the heat of the sun, even though she also knew that he was doing what he'd done before. Distracting her to take her mind off her objections to a fake engagement party that he wasn't going to veto because this further descent into deceit didn't bother him.

Her body stiffening, where before it had been weakly melding with his, she fisted her hands against his chest and pushed. 'I'm warning you—if that fake party goes ahead, I won't be there!'

'Neither will I, *cara*.'

Her smooth brow furrowed at that, her hot words swallowed. Was he going to put a stop to it after all? It seemed like it. Gradually her fists unfurled, her palms lying against his chest where she could feel the steady beat of his heart, the heat of his skin beneath the soft fabric of his collarless shirt.

Brilliant golden eyes searched hers. Her breasts felt heavy and her skin tingled as a shameful heat coiled deep inside her, intensifying as one of his hands slid down her body to rest against the curve of her hip.

She tensed. Did he know what he was doing to her? Did he care? Probably not! She was just some fluttery female he could bend to his will with the effortless expenditure of just a little of that overwhelming sexual appeal of his! And yet—

'What do you mean?' With a determined effort to get

out of the danger zone she wriggled away, but he simply placed a strong lean hand on the small of her back and hauled her back again. Her breath was expelled in a gasp at the close contact with his powerful body, and her words were little more than a ragged whisper when she pressed on, with difficulty, 'You said you wouldn't be at the party, either.'

Hoisting himself up on one elbow, his eyes gleaming between their fringing of thick dark lashes, he smiled at her before lowering his proud head to take her lush pink mouth with his, stroking with a sensuality that made her whimper and quiver before he imparted, 'We won't attend a fake engagement party, my Lily. I want it to be a real one.' And, as her eyes widened in bewilderment, he said. 'I'm asking you to marry me.'

CHAPTER EIGHT

LILY stared at him in shock. She opened her mouth to speak but no words came out.

Paolo simply smiled with sheer male complacency as he gently threaded his fingers through her silky-soft hair and positioned her to meet his exact requirements. He lowered his dark head and murmured against the moist softness of her lush pink mouth, 'You will be my bride, Lily,' with all the innate self-assurance of the alpha male who always got what he demanded, and for whom pleading or even merely asking nicely was foreign to his dynamic nature.

That type of arrogant domination shouldn't turn her bones to water and her skin to fire, make her ache to submit, but it did. And, much as she deplored it, there was nothing she could do about it.

With helpless resignation she was excruciatingly aware of the coil of stinging heat deep in the pit of her stomach, the insistently urgent straining of her breasts beneath the thin cotton top she was wearing—aware, to her everlasting shame, that Paolo Venini only had to touch her and she was aroused to such a peak of sexual excitement, of loving and longing, that she forgot everything—who she was, who he was, her common sense and self-respect, everything she valued about herself.

Desperate to get the word *no* beyond the tight constriction of her throat, all she managed was a quivering moan of instinctive response as he parted her lips with his and began a totally erotic assault on her senses. His tongue plunged into the inner yielding sweetness with raw masculine urgency and his hands slipped beneath the soft fabric of her top, his groan of satisfaction telling her befuddled brain that the discovery she was braless did more than merely please him.

As deft hands pushed her top up, exposing her straining pink-crested breasts to his simmering gaze, Lily made a furious effort to pull herself together, fighting the need to surrender to this man she loved more than she'd thought possible.

Squirming away from him, shaking, her face flushed and troubled, she managed, 'This is madness!'

At that a slow smile softened his sculpted features, and his golden eyes, hazed over with the smoke of desire, crinkled at the corners as he breathed, 'If this is madness, then I like it. I like it more than I can say, *cara*! I can't get enough of it!'

And he closed her to him again, and this time his kiss was filled with fiery passion, robbing her of breath and sanity. Only when they came up for long-denied air could

Lily get out on a shaky gasp, 'Why would you want to marry when you've already told me you hate the idea?'

She pushed self-protectively away from him, privately thanking her guardian angel for allowing her that much strength of mind. And he let her. He had to have some ulterior motive for that insane proposal. She hadn't a clue what it was, knew only that it had to be cruel, because she was already hurting.

'Don't tell me you've fallen in love with me!' she managed unevenly.

And she despised herself for what he must see as the pall of disappointment that covered her expressive features as he took one of her hands and countered, 'What is falling in love? Just a sanitising phrase to make the basic urge of lust seem more acceptable.' He trapped her hand with lean bronzed fingers. 'I freely admit to lust—you turn me on, you make me burn, you touch me on a deeper level than any woman has ever done, *cara mia*. I know you too are desperate for our lovemaking, the way you respond tells me this, but I also know you are not mistress material. You are sweet and innocent, and I would not demean you by asking you to share my bed without marriage.'

There was unhidden male appreciation in his warm golden gaze now. 'Therefore, I have changed my mind about marriage. It would not be such a bad thing.'

With one fluid movement he reached for her again and tumbled her back onto the herb-scented grass, that tormenting hand slipping beneath her top to explore her

unbearably sensitised breasts, sending a fireball of eroti-
cism scorching through her.

His wickedly sensual mouth was a whisper away
from her trembling lips as he murmured urgently,
'Marriage. Think of it, my Lily. Being able to enjoy your
delightful body, giving you pleasure with an easy conscience, caring for you, pleasing Mamma instead of
having to present her with a broken engagement at some
time in the future.' His hand was now sliding down to
the soft curve of her tummy, making her weak with
longing—until he asked on a thickened growl, 'What
could be more convenient?'

Convenient!

For him!

Give Fiora what she wanted, make her happy. Allow
him to slake his self-admitted lust until she bored him
as, with his track record, she surely must.

And what about me? she wanted to howl, but didn't.
No point in letting him see how deeply he could hurt her.
Allowing him to guess that she'd fallen in love with him.
Adding several more cubic metres to that already
massive ego of his!

His insulting proposal was all about doing his duty by
his mother and slaking his newly discovered lust for
someone he had termed an innocent. The way he'd talked
about bedding her with an easy conscience made her pretty
darn sure he'd never had sex with a virgin before.

And how did he know she was a virgin—an 'innocent'?
Was it that obvious? Was she that gauche?

Well, the novelty of bedding a virgin would soon wear off, Lily knew. Tears stung at the backs of her eyes. He had a low boredom threshold. She knew that, too. He would tire of her, as he'd tired of his first wife, and she'd be shuffled off, hidden away, forgotten. Broken?

Not even the short-lived ecstasy of being his novel new wife would compensate for that sort of hurt.

But not for anything would she let him guess at the emotions that were threatening to pull her apart. Give him the smallest hint of how she really felt about him and he'd move in for the kill! And, knowing how weak she was where he was concerned, she'd make a very willing victim!

Taking a deep breath, she called on every last scrap of her will-power and told him, more or less levelly, 'I won't marry you, Paolo. I'm flattered. I think. But it's not going to happen.'

Steeling herself for another determined assault on her senses, she was left bewildered and perhaps, she thought, with more than a little self-disgust, disappointed as he slowly released her.

He was on his feet with enviable ease, his hands thrust deep into the pockets of his cargo pants, his smile frighteningly assured. 'Then, *cara*, I have two more days before the party to change your mind. Don't stay out in the sun too long. Even at this time of year delicate skins can burn.'

Somehow Lily managed to avoid Paolo until dinner that evening. Cook had excelled herself, with lobster in a light sauce followed by caramelised grapes, but she was barely able to swallow more than a mouthful of each.

Forcing herself to keep up with Fiora's lively chatter on the dreaded subject of the coming engagement party was the only way she could deflect attention from her lack of appetite. Inside she was wound up tight, fit to blow at any moment.

As for Paolo—well, she didn't dare look at him. But she felt him watching her, and from his occasional lazy comments she knew he understood how she was struggling to avoid his gaze, and was mightily amused by it.

Because—

Because he knew as well as she did that he only had to exert a fraction of the sexual magnetism he possessed in spades to have her helpless, completely in his power, agreeing to anything he demanded of her—even a marriage she knew would end in bitter failure.

And it scared her silly!

She wanted him—wanted to be his wife more than she'd ever wanted anything before. The offer was there, but she couldn't take it.

With the evidence of one broken engagement, one short-lived marriage and countless casual affairs behind him, she would be committing emotional suicide if she gave in to temptation. If he loved her she would be the happiest woman on the planet. But he didn't. He'd said as much. And she wasn't prepared to have her heart broken.

She wasn't that recklessly stupid, was she?

Diving into a tiny gap in the on-going conversation

around the table, Lily asked in a thin, tight voice she didn't recognise as her own, 'Fiora, could you spare Carla for a short while tomorrow morning? I need to go into Florence—without Paolo. I'd like to buy him a betrothal gift!' She forced a smile to hide her dismay at yet another miserable lie, her heart rattling. 'If she could drive me in, I could find my own way back.'

She held her breath, fully expecting him to offer to drive her himself. He'd know the betrothal gift was pure fabrication and smell a rat. Know she was avoiding his company at all costs because she was terrified of his stated intention to make her change her mind about accepting his proposal before the guests arrived for the wretched party.

But all he said was, 'Mario shall drive you, *cara*. Just tell him what time you wish to return and he will come for you. Spend all day exploring our beautiful city, if that is what you want. But as for a betrothal gift—all I need is your sweet self, you know that. However, if it pleases you to choose something, a small gift to mark the occasion, then I, of course, will be delighted.'

Louse! What was he playing at? He would know that her sudden desire to go into town was an avoiding tactic. That she didn't trust herself when faced with his devastating brand of 'persuasion'. She might love him, but she would never understand him in a million years!

She did look at him then, and the perfection of his features took her breath away. The slow, sexy smile he gave her worked its usual havoc. Her breath catching,

she excused herself, pleading a slight headache, and
headed for the sanctuary of her room, locking the door
behind her. Just in case.

Florence was an assault on Lily's already reeling senses.
So much beauty, so much style, it was difficult to take
in—especially as she felt in need of an enormous ball
of string in order to find herself back in the square where
Mario had dropped her off and had promised to collect
her at five in the afternoon.

Footsore, but slightly easier in her mind after time
alone, without the fear that Paolo might find her and
work that special magic that could make her resolve
melt like ice on a summer's day, Lily made it back to
the meeting place with half an hour to spare. Tables
outside a trattoria provided an excuse to sit in the shade,
and the espresso she ordered was more than welcome.

Dismissing the occasional feeling that she was being
followed as paranoia, she knew what she had to do.

Just this evening and tomorrow to make sure she
didn't give Paolo the opportunity to use all his formidable powers of persuasion, and then hopefully the
arrival of his mother's guests on the following day
would severely limit their time alone together.

And so she'd be at the fake engagement so-called
celebration. She couldn't carry out her earlier stated intention to boycott it because that would upset Fiora, and
she didn't want to do that, but after that she'd be off. She
would have to manufacture some urgently pressing

reason for an immediate return to England. She didn't know what, but she'd think of something.

'*Signorina*—you are ready?'

Blinking, Lily glanced at the slim young man in dark trousers and immaculate white shirt. Mario. Exactly on time. Suspicion solidified into certainty.

She rose, collected her bag. 'Have you been following me, Mario?'

'*Certamente.* The *signor* instructed it.' He grinned widely, lifting narrow shoulders. 'You are precious to him. No harm must come to you.'

Fuming, Lily stalked across the *piazza* to where the gleaming car was waiting, Mario trailing in her wake. So much for her hours of freedom! In spite of what Mario thought, this was *not* about caring, anxiety for her well-being. It was all about Paolo's control. She had become his property, she realised with a sinking feeling. Followed. Watched. And no doubt he would demand a detailed report of what she'd been doing, she thought with ire.

But it wasn't Mario's fault. He had only done what he'd been told to do by the all-powerful Paolo Venini. So she was able to keep up a light-hearted conversation as they journeyed back through the Tuscan countryside, her mind working on another level as she formulated exactly what she would say on the subject of people with nasty suspicious minds who put minders on the tail of other people!

More than ever convinced that her only option was to return to England as soon as she'd done her duty by

Fiora and been put on show at the wretched party, she decided, with deep reluctance, that she would have to compound her sins and lie again. Say Great-Aunt Edith was ill and really needed her.

It was utterly distasteful, but it was the only thing she could think of that Fiora would understand. She would be disappointed that her visit was to be cut short, the plans for the wedding put on hold for a while, but she would understand and sympathise with the need.

And it would be up to Paolo to confess that the wedding was off at a time of his choosing!

The high she experienced at having thought herself out of the mess lasted until the car drew to a well-bred halt in front of the villa.

Then crumbled into hopelessness as she saw Paolo, looking heart-stoppingly gorgeous in slim-fitting denims and a white T-shirt, emerge from the open doorway, an all too healthy Great-Aunt Edith smiling fit to split her face at his side.

Her last escape route had been well and truly blocked by that dramatically handsome grinning devil!

CHAPTER NINE

IT WAS almost as if he'd read her mind even before she'd worked out her escape strategy, Lily thought, near to hysterics as she advanced on suddenly shaky legs towards the now broadly grinning pair, asking baldly, 'How did *you* get here?'

'What a welcome, child!'

To her astonishment Lily found herself crushed against her great-aunt's stout bosom in a rare show of open affection. 'By private jet and helicopter! Just imagine—I felt like royalty! Paolo arranged everything!'

'We couldn't celebrate our engagement without her,' came his unwelcome cool assertion.

Extricating herself from the bear-hug, Lily shot him a look of loathing. He gave her back a smile of simmering amusement, shot through with the satisfaction of a male who made things happen to get what he wanted.

No wonder he hadn't raised any objections over her awayday—he'd just put one of his staff on her tail and set about finalising the arrangements for the transportation of her elderly relative, in doing so making sure she, Lily, was put into an even more difficult situation! Ruthless and manipulative wasn't in it!

'I've been so excited since dear Paolo phoned with the news of your engagement!' Edith exclaimed warmly. 'And I don't think I've slept a wink since he invited me to come here and stay for the wedding!'

Oh, yes, he had her thoroughly outmanoeuvred.

'Why don't we go round to the terrace? Agata will provide us with cold drinks,' Paolo slid in, velvet-smooth. 'Mamma is resting before dinner. She might believe she is one hundred per cent fit, but she is still frail,' he added, with a detectable note of warning aimed at her, Lily realised with helpless rage.

He had no need to remind her of Fiora's delicate health, Lily thought darkly. She had grown genuinely fond of his mother, and if it hadn't been for her own un-willingness to distress her unduly she would have left Italy the moment she'd acknowledged she'd done the unthinkable and fallen in love with a man who was so wrong for her—valid excuse or not!

Fiora's continuing recovery from her life-threatening illness was his strongest bargaining tool. And now he'd brought her great-aunt in on the act, giving him another. She could kill the manipulating devil!

Her eyes boring into his broad back as they walked round to the side of the immense villa, she barely registered Edith's, 'I hope I didn't tire her. We had such a long and interesting chat after I arrived. Forgive me if I kept her too long.'

Arrested by the anxious note, Paolo turned, his smile warmly sincere as he swiftly reassured her. 'You are Lily's family, Edith—and Mamma prizes family relationships above all. Her retirement had nothing to do with your more than welcome presence, I promise. Carla, her companion, and I always insist that she rests each afternoon. Meeting you, having you here, makes her happy. And happiness is the best medicine, yes?'

Another none too subtle warning for her, Lily fulminated as they passed beneath the long pergola, festooned and dripping with wistaria, and headed for the steps that led up to the broad terrace.

As soon as she got her great-aunt on her own she would have to confess that the engagement—as far as she was concerned—was a total sham. Explain what had led up to this sorry situation. She wasn't looking forward to it. There was no one more upright and straightforward than her relative, and she would rightly deplore the deceit and make no bones about saying so!

But the opportunity was lost when Paolo left them to go in search of the housekeeper. Edith immediately turned to her, her eyes over-bright with emotion, and declared, 'I can't tell you how happy your news has made me, child! Such a weight off my mind! I must confess that I have worried about your future well-being for some time now. No—hear me out,' she demanded, as Lily opened her mouth to protest. 'I won't be around for ever, and who knows what has become of your feckless father. I hated to think of you being left alone in the world.'

She gravitated to a table in the shade and ordered, with just a hint of her old asperity, 'Sit. Don't hover, child. I *have* worried about you,' she stressed. 'Working all hours for little reward save that of knowing you were helping people who needed it. No opportunity or time to meet a suitable young man or embark on a financially rewarding career. I blamed myself for being so bound up in Life Begins and not giving a thought to your future. Not doing nearly enough for you.'

'Don't talk like that!' Lily cried emotionally. 'You'll be around for ages yet! And you did *everything* for me,' she protested with vehemence, distressed at what she was hearing, adding with heartfelt sympathy, 'It can't have been easy.' At a time when most women would have been thinking of slowing down, taking things a little easier, Edith had taken in a baby that had been as good as abandoned. 'You gave me family, a feeling of belonging, a happy and secure childhood.'

'It was never difficult, child. Never!' Edith's eyes grew moist with rare sentiment. 'And now I need no longer worry. News of your forthcoming wedding has taken a huge weight off my shoulders, believe me! Such a strong, caring man—so much wealth…' She waved an expressive hand at their surroundings. 'Mind you, were he as poor as a church mouse I would still heartily approve. Whatever his financial situation he would make any woman a fine husband. As it is, his gene-rosity means that we can safely leave the future of Life Begins in capable hands, so that's one more anxiety laid to rest.'

Paolo didn't rejoin them. Agata, bringing iced fresh orange juice, imparted that the *signor* sent his regrets. He had work to do and would see them at dinner.

Leaving her great-aunt in her room, exclaiming over the amenities and deciding which of her two dresses was more suitable for the coming dinner, Lily set out to look for him. Fit to spit tacks. What right had he to go behind her back and bring her unsuspecting great-aunt into this mess of his?

He was good at humiliating her—wasn't he just? She'd thought she'd been so clever—avoiding him and his threatened 'persuasion'—but all the time he'd had all the aces up his sleeve, had been laughing at her. No wonder he'd allowed her to go out of her way to avoid him!

Marching straight into the room he used as a study, she found him standing by the tall window using his cellphone. Shifting from foot to foot, she waited until he had finished the call, refusing to let herself be im-pressed by his dark male magnificence, her eyes still spitting sparks of rage when he turned to her and smiled.

'How dare you?' She launched straight in, practi-cally bouncing up and down in her need to go over there and slap him.

'*Cara?*' One perfectly shaped dark eyebrow arched in a query Lily found totally exasperating.

'You *know* what I'm talking about!' Bright spots of anger flared on her cheeks. 'You *know* what you've done. Now there'll be two old ladies to disappoint instead of one! Have you any idea—? Do you know what she said to me? She said knowing my future's secure—huh!—has taken a huge load off her mind!'

Eyes glittering, she was almost incoherent with rage that he had put her in this dreadful situation. 'You use people like pawns to get what you want. You never consider their feelings,' she accused wildly.

With difficulty Paolo stopped himself from grinning from ear to ear. Little Lily Frome was a bewitching delight. A small bundle of hissing fury!

It took courage to stand there and bad-mouth him, he acknowledged with renewed admiration. Used as he was to everyone—especially the bed partners who were now definitely history—treating him as if he were some kind of god, bending over backwards to please him, feeding him servile flattery, Lily in confrontational mood made him feel fully, vitally alive for the first time in years.

'I do what needs to be done. Haven't you heard the saying that the end justifies the means?'

As Lily watched him move towards her she felt stifled. The air locked in her lungs. Her small hands fisted. 'The end'—he meant marriage.

To her!

Not because he loved her. As if! But because it would

be convenient. Not wanting to disappoint his mother because he adored her, and after the tragedy that had taken his brother, his sister-in-law and their unborn child, he would do anything to make her remaining years contented. And, hey, bedding a virgin would be a novel experience. He could teach her everything he knew about sexual pleasure. Until he grew bored!

Thanks, but no thanks! She might love him, warts and all, and lust after him until it became a burning ache she could barely contain, but she had too much self-respect to allow herself to accept his insulting proposal.

And he was now close. Too close. Even so, she found the will to jerk her chin up at a defiant angle and meet his eyes.

Big mistake!

The smouldering mesmeric quality, the glittering golden lights, made her feel light-headed. He always had that effect on her, she mourned in silent self-contempt. And when he took one of her hands and uncurled her fingers she could do nothing to stop him.

Stroking her palm with one lean finger, he cracked down on the urgency of his desire to carry her over to the couch, strip her, reveal again the tantalising all-woman nakedness that had already been open to his avid view. To slide eager, questing hands over every delightful curve and hollow of her small but exquisitely proportioned body, discover the secret heart of her femininity and pleasure her until she was begging for release. To make her his.

But she was to be his wife. He was determined on that. And as his future wife she commanded his respect. Thrusting aside the erotic fantasies, promising himself that they would be played out in full on their wedding night, he said thickly, 'No one needs to be disappointed, *cara mia*. Our marriage will make everyone happy.'

Such rampant sex appeal was dangerous. She felt hot, restless, her breasts tight, the nipples pushing against the thin camisole top she was wearing beneath an elegant linen suit, and her mind had been reduced to a fuzzy blank—apart from the tiny voice that was urging her to give in, do anything he wanted her to do, admit she loved him. Then the realisation that he was manipulating her again brought her to her senses as effectively as if he'd tossed a bucket of icy water over her.

Snatching back her hand, she took a step away, a pulse beating furiously at her temples. He was working on her soft nature. Clever enough to understand that she would hate hurting anyone she loved. He knew how fond she and Fiora were of each other. Knew she cared deeply for her great-aunt, valued all she'd done for her, the sacrifices she'd made when she'd adopted her, brought her up as if she were her own child.

Well, she'd show him she wasn't as soft as he obviously thought she was. Her chin high, she got out, 'You forgot me when you listed the people who would find happiness through our marriage. Or was I supposed to be included in "everyone"?'

Scorn for his methods, when all he had to do was say

he loved her and mean it, which she knew would never happen, gave her the strength to walk out, telling him, 'I *won't* marry you. I'll leave you to break the bad news in your own time and carry the results on your own conscience—if you have one!'

Lily gazed at her reflection with no enthusiasm. She was wearing the smoky blue backless designer gown—minus underwear—hoping it would make her feel more like a grown woman with a mind of her own rather than a doll in the hands of an expert puppet-master.

It wasn't working. Her mind, what was left of it, was being jerked every which way. Her adamant decision to reject Paolo's proposal out of hand was wavering, then veering back on track again, until something else happened to swing it right back in the other direction.

The latest being the shattering conversation she'd had with her great-aunt a couple of hours ago.

'I want to talk to you.' The old lady's whisper had been loud enough to singe her ears. 'It's not necessary, but I'd like your agreement.'

Wondering what Edith was on about, Lily had found herself in the small salon that overlooked the gardens at the rear of the villa, the door closed firmly behind them, the old lady peering round to make sure they were alone. 'You know Fiora and her companion plan to move back to her home in Florence immediately following the wedding? Well, what do you think of this?' She'd pulled in a big breath, then added on a rush, 'I'm invited to move here to Italy—make my home in Florence with them! Such a lovely city, I believe. I've always wanted to see it, but never could afford the time or the pennies to do it!'

Speechless at that heart-sinking announcement, Lily could only stare into her beloved great-aunt's glowing eyes.

'Cat got your tongue?'

'I—' Struggling to get her head around this latest development, Lily didn't know where to start. 'What about your cottage—the charity?' But she knew what the answer would be.

It came as expected. 'The charity's fine—more part-time volunteers than ever, splendid fundraising activities planned, Paolo's support. And as for the cottage—it goes to you in my will. But married to Paolo you won't need it. So I shall sell it and pay my way in Florence with the proceeds.'

Her heart some miles beneath her feet, Lily said, 'So you've made your mind up?'

'As good as. Fiora and I get on like a house on fire. I wouldn't consider the move if we didn't. Apparently her apartment is enormous, fully staffed. And we'd be company for each other. Carla's splendid, but Fiora says she often longs for someone nearer her own age to talk with. And of course I'd be near to you—not that I'd be forever visiting and being a nuisance, but I'd be near.'

And, as if Lily's wide-eyed stare was not the enthusiastic reception she'd expected, the old lady had added confidently, 'Paolo's opinion has been sought. He thinks it's a splendid idea!'

I just bet he does! Lily thought now, heartily sick of everything being 'splendid', and turning from the mirror. Outmanoeuvred again! If she persisted in her refusal to marry Paolo those happy plans would bite the dust.

Great-Aunt Edith had a strong, unshakable sense of duty. She would no more go ahead with her plans to move to Florence, sell the cottage to fund her life here and in the process see her, Lily, homeless or living in a bedsit, than sprout wings and fly. They would move back to England and take up the life they had left.

Could she be selfish enough to deny the old lady the luxury and ease she deserved in her declining years?

Edith had never married. A teacher for many years, she had founded the small local charity and adopted her great-niece on her retirement from full-time employment at the age of sixty, having worked hard all her life with precious few of life's small luxuries. Didn't she deserve something much better now?

And, to make everything so much worse, Paolo had been so warm, so attentive—respectful, even—during the last couple of days. The perfect Italian fiancé. On the one hand it had made her fall more deeply in love with him, and on the other it made her feel decidedly murderous!

Looking forward to this evening's engagement party with as much pleasure as she would if faced with an appointment with her dentist for root canal work, she heaved a heartfelt sigh and slipped her feet into high-heeled mules.

The guests would be waiting for the happy couple to put in an appearance. Her stomach gave a violent lurch. Apparently a handful of Paolo's closest friends had been invited and, ominously, the village priest. And the cousins, of course. Three males and a female. They'd arrived an hour ago, but she'd only had time to smile wanly, register the males with sharp suits and indolent attitudes, and a striking Latin beauty who looked bored, before they'd been shown to their respective rooms.

On reflection, she thought she could sympathise with Paolo for having little time for them, but grumbled at herself for being uncharitable enough to condemn on first sight a bunch of people who were probably perfectly nice.

Nervously twisting the heavy ring on her finger, she straightened her spine. She couldn't hide in her room any longer. Time to face them and take part in this distasteful charade. Try to stop going over and over the uncomfortable facts that in refusing to marry Paolo she would distress her great-aunt, casting a pall of disappointment over her remaining years—not to forget Fiora, who would be one very unhappy lady.

As if her anguished thoughts, centred on the impossible male who was the author of all her present troubles, had conjured him up, Paolo entered the room.

Lily's progress towards the door skidded to a halt. In his white dinner jacket he was breathtakingly handsome, his hard male mouth softened into that sensual smile that always took her wits and scattered them.

Covering the space between them in a couple of fluid strides, his eyes holding her, entrapping her, he took her hand and lifted it to his lips, confidence oozing from every pore as he commented, 'You look spectacular, *cara mia*. A future bride any man would be proud to claim.' He held her hand against his broad chest, tugging her closer with a gentleness that almost defeated her, making her deplore the weakness that urged her to lean into him, to cling and never let go. But then he claimed, 'Not too long ago you accused me of considering everyone's happiness but yours—'

Which gave her the strength of mind to counter, 'And considering only your convenience—'

'Let me speak.' His voice lowered to a spine-weakening husky promise. 'I could make you happy. I will make you happy,' he stressed in amendment, and Lily sucked in a shaky breath, hypnotised by his golden eyes, by the lean, olive-toned male beauty of his unforgettable features, horrified by her internal admission that, yes, he could make her happy.

Ecstatically happy.

For about a week.

Until she bored him. And she was left broken, like his first wife.

Denying herself the relief of flinging her head back and wailing like a baby deprived of its most treasured plaything, she pushed out, 'We don't want to keep the guests waiting, do we?' and headed for the door. She paused just long enough to take a deep breath and make sure her voice emerged sounding as if she were in control. Of herself. Of everything. 'You may be king fish in the pond you swim in, but I will not be forced or emotionally blackmailed into doing something I know would be wrong for me—something I don't want to do.'

Then was undone as his arm snaked around her narrow waist, his warm breath feathering her ear as he whispered, 'But you *do* want to do it, my sweet Lily. And if I had the time I would prove it to you now.'

Her face flaming, Lily leant against him, needing his support because her legs had gone hollow, her whole body weakened by the shameful hunger he could awake in her effortlessly. Miserably aware, as they went down to greet the guests, that she was fighting a battle on two fronts.

With him. And, more terrifyingly, with herself.

CHAPTER TEN

PAOLO leant against the frame of the open French
windows, one hand in the pocket of his narrowly cut
black trousers, the collar of his dress shirt undone, the
shimmering gold of his eyes partly veiled by an enviably
thick fringe of black lashes.

Watching her.

Lily's delicate loveliness drew every eye in the room,
and the dress she was wearing made him so hot for her
he couldn't wait for this tedious party to be over and he
could take a long cold shower.

Overturning his long-held rejection of the idea of re-
marriage had been the right thing to do, he congratulated
himself, his eyes following her as she and the wife of one
of his oldest friends moved out of the way of a couple who
were dancing to music pounding out from the state-of-
the-art stereo system. Cousin Orfeo's idea, he supposed,
suppressing vague irritation. Fortunately the grand salon
had been largely cleared, and could accommodate those
of the guests who chose to indulge in the pointless activity.

With ease he dismissed his notoriously workshy, playboy cousin, and returned his mind to a far more pleasant subject.

Marriage to Lily, who didn't treat him with tedious simpering deference, who didn't have a greedy eye on the main chance, as proved beyond all doubt by her rejection of his proposal when every other woman he knew would have tied herself in knots to accept such an offer, was the obvious step to take. It would be of indisputable benefit to all concerned, an entirely logical step. And logic—not emotional muddle—was how he liked to live his life.

He would no longer have to endure the constant feeling of guilt because his former refusal to settle down and sire an heir and a spare was causing his mother a great deal of grief—even more so since Antonio's death.

He would have a wife and companion he could trust implicitly, and in return Lily would have status, his care and fidelity, his children.

A band tightened about his heart at that entirely novel prospect. And the hope that their first child would be a girl, small and delicately formed, with those huge silvery grey eyes just like Lily's, hit him like a thunderclap.

Unused to bracketing himself and children together, he found the picture pretty startling. He shifted his feet and decided that he liked the idea. At least, he amended, with Lily as the mother of his children he liked the idea.

His eyes narrowed. She was being approached now by his cousin Renata. Lazy, like the rest of the clan, offspring of his father's unlamented, light-fingered brother, and believing the world owed her a living. Greedy, bitchy.

Still watching, he twitched his long mouth. Lily didn't know it, but her over-emphasised refusal to be his wife was soon to be turned on its head. Everything was in place. The arrival of her relative, planned and executed with precision, had set the scene. The unlooked-for but fortuitous liking the two senior ladies had quickly formed for each other, and their consequent decision to share the apartment in Florence, had been the icing on the cake, the last nail in the coffin of Lily's resistance— proof, if he needed it, that the gods were on his side.

Tomorrow he would take Lily to his villa in the hills above Amalfi. Alone with him, she wouldn't be able to hold out, resist his powers of persuasion. He had been around long enough to know when a woman was sexually attracted to him, and she was. He'd read the signs. Her days of digging her heels in were numbered! And to his dying day he wouldn't let her regret it.

He had done his duty as a host, circulating, receiving congratulations on his betrothal, had danced attendance on his mother and Edith. In a moment he would claim his Lily, make sure he mentioned the visit to Amalfi in front of his mother and Edith, certain that she wouldn't make a scene and refuse to go anywhere with him, because he knew that she was already beating herself up over the prospect of having to sorely disappoint the two women some time in the near future.

Which worked to his advantage, but made him

deeply uncomfortable. When it came right down to it he didn't like himself for playing on her caring nature, for manipulating her. But it would be for the best in the long run. Her life with him would be happy, and she would want for nothing. He would make sure of that.

A sudden scowl darkened his eyes. Lily, turning white-faced away from Renata, had brushed against his cousin Orfeo, who promptly swept her unresisting body into his arms and into a clumsy parody of a foxtrot.

His stubby fingers were splayed over the unblemished creamy skin of her back, sliding down her delicate spine and dipping beneath the barrier of fabric. His oiled-looking head pressed against hers as he whispered something.

Murderous rage surged through Paolo. How dared that oily creep paw *his* woman?

He strode forward.

She was hating every second of this. The congratulations, the curious looks veiled with sycophantic smiles, the whole wretched lying charade she'd got herself caught up in. And, worst of all, the radiantly happy smiles of Fiora and her great-aunt as they sat chatting together at a table in an alcove.

Worst of all, that was, until Paolo's cousin Renata slid up to her, a glass of red wine clutched in long white fingers, almost wearing a dress of sequinned scarlet.

'Nice work!' she said. 'You've nailed the wealthiest man in Italy—probably in the whole of Europe. It won't last, of course, but think of the big fat settlement you'll get when he decides marriage bores him!' She gave a tinkling laugh as brittle as breaking glass. 'Dear Paolo the heartbreaker. He has the attention span of a gnat when it comes to the female sex—fact, I'm afraid. He can't help it! His first wife got the elbow after only a few months. She overdosed, you know, only a few months after they broke up. Some say it was deliberate.' She shrugged, as if disassociating herself from the slander. 'For your sake, let's hope you're made of sterner stuff!'

Refusing to dignify that piece of malicious spite with a response, Lily turned away, feeling sick at what the other woman had implied. To her huge annoyance she found herself swept into the centre of the room by another of Paolo's cousins.

Dancing was the very last thing she wanted to do. She wanted to escape the noise, the pointed questions and speculative looks, the pervasive scent of the banks of flowers that seemed to be everywhere. Switch her mind off and stop fretting over this horrible situation. Just for a little while. Just until she found the strength she'd need to tell her great-aunt and Fiora the truth.

And the wretched man was actually *pawing* her! The crudities he was murmuring in her ear disgusted her, and as she tried to pull away his hot, heavy hand slid down to her waist and hauled her into him. The aftershave he must have drenched himself in made her feel as if she were about to throw up.

'Beat it, Orfeo!'

Never had Lily been so glad to see Paolo. Her anger with him for putting her in such an unenviable situation vanished like mist in the sunlight.

She felt weak with love, totally debilitated with longing, her mind—what was left of it—in so much turmoil she felt as if her brain had been boiled!

She wanted so much to be with him, accept his proposal. But she knew she couldn't. Mustn't.

Her knees shook as he slipped an arm around her shoulders, and, trying to stiffen her already tottery resolve, she took a moment to remind herself that given what she knew about him—what appeared to be general knowledge—marrying him would be self-destructive madness.

Yet Paolo Venini looked as if he would tear the younger man into pieces, limb from limb. Outrage had darkened his eyes to blazing ice. Looking up into his hard, rivetingly handsome features, she felt her eyes well with feeble tears.

'Don't let that lowlife upset you, *cara mia*,' he urged as the younger man sloped away, tugging at his tie in red-faced humiliation. 'If he comes within a hundred miles of you again I will kill him! Him or any man who shows you disrespect!'

Her soft mouth wobbled into a smile. Almost she could believe him. But did that mean he was jealous? He had his faults, but she had never numbered possessiveness among them. Where his women were concerned his *modus operandi* seemed to be to take what he wanted for as long as his interest lasted, then throw the current female aside and forget her. Move on. Not really the actions of a man with a possessive streak.

Paolo dropped his protective arm and curved a hand around her waist. 'Come with me, *bella mia*. We will escape together.' Time enough later to take her to sit with Fiora and Edith and mention the trip to Amalfi. Right now Lily was looking stressed, and she needed to unwind. That—her well-being—was his first priority. 'No one will miss us, and if they do they will understand the need of a newly betrothed couple to be alone together, to take time out for a few minutes.'

A danger light flashed its warning, but Lily recklessly ignored it as he guided her through the open French windows. As the cooler, soft night air enfolded them Lily leant into the strength of his lean, toned body. Needed to.

This was what she needed, she decided, on a rush of relief at having left the party behind, as he led her down a grassy path, the sound of music, chatter and laughter thankfully receding.

Tonight had been a nightmare. Her emotions all over the place. With him at her side as he'd introduced her to the guests she'd felt wired to the point of detonation, stingingly aware of every breath he took, every movement he made. When he'd left her to circulate on her own she'd felt bereft. Weak. The self-protective need to resist him fading to nothing.

Such had been her emotionally muddled state that she'd actually been on the point of searching the room to find him and tell him she *would* marry him. Partly for

Fiora's and Great-Aunt Edith's sake, but mostly, she knew, because she couldn't bear the thought of never seeing him again. Then that dreadful woman had come up to her and spilt out her spite. Spite that had a firm basis in fact, reminding her that Paolo would never love her, just use her to ease his conscience where his mother was concerned. She didn't know how she could love a man like that. But, for her sins, she did.

She bit down hard on her lower lip, annoyed with herself. Her brain was hurting. She didn't want to think of any of it, wanted just to close her mind and enjoy this brief period of silent tranquillity.

'You are quiet, my Lily.' His voice was like a caress, setting tiny shivers to sensitise her skin.

'I've switched my mind off,' she confessed.

She registered his amused, 'Ah—that I can understand!' just loving being this close to him. Strangely, she felt unthreatened now. He had rescued her from that pawing idiot back there, whisked her away from all those curious stares, from his friends and family probably trying to work out how plain, ordinary her had snared a guy who was so anti-marriage it was legend. Did they all think, as that creepy cousin of his had crudely suggested, that she was so fantastic in bed that he had to hang on to her? The very thought made her go hot all over.

All she wanted to do was not think of any of it, make a renewed effort to empty her stubborn mind of all those knotty problems and enjoy the silence and the solitude.

He was matching his pace to hers, not talking, his arm around her waist, thankfully keeping his mouth shut on the subject of marriage—because right now she was sure she couldn't handle it.

His hand resting on the curve of her hip felt so right. The air was full of the gentle scent of the flowers and wild herbs of the hillside, the moonlight gleaming on the stands of silvery eucalyptus, turning the night to the sort of soft magic that talking would destroy.

Determined that nothing would come between her and this so desperately needed period of tranquillity, she didn't protest, didn't even think of trying to when, at the end of a path she hadn't explored before, they came across a summerhouse festooned in climbing roses in early bud.

'We will sit a while.' Leading her to a wide padded bench seat that ran along the full length of the far wall, he eased her down, laid a hand against the side of her face, turning her head so that he could see her eyes in the dim silvery light. 'I didn't see you relax with a drink in your hand all evening. Would you like me to phone through to the house and have someone bring us champagne?'

Instinctively nuzzling into his hand, she let a smile thread her voice as she said, 'Such decadence! Thank you, but no. I don't need to have alcohol to relax.' She didn't add that being with him here, like this, was intoxicating enough. She'd been arguing with him ever since they'd met and she was tired of it. Just for a few moments—until they returned to the villa and normal battle-ready positions were resumed—she wanted to sink into this feeling of real closeness.

For some reason her answer seemed to please him. She felt him smile. Now, how could that be? Could she really be that closely attuned to him? she pondered, with a little shiver of awe.

'You are cold?' His voice had a strange rough edge as he turned her head towards him. Moonlight bathed them with a faint silvery glow, casting his features into harsh relief, all planes and angles, but his eyes were soft—what she could see of them before he dipped his head and used his sensual mouth to close one pale eyelid and then the other, his lips drifting down to lay a feather-light kiss on one corner of her mouth.

Without understanding how it happened, only that it had to, Lily's lips parted as she sought his teasing mouth. She loved his kisses, and taking one tonight couldn't be wrong—could it?

He laced his long fingers in her hair as he took her soft pink lips in a kiss that knocked out her senses, promised heaven, made her feel fully alive and yet weak with hunger for him all at the same time.

Her hands came up to cling to his broad shoulders for support, her peaking breasts pressed against the cool fabric of his shirt, and she felt him stiffen, a tremor racing through his perfectly honed body as he lifted his mouth from hers.

A tiny mew of frustration escaped her. She felt like a starving orphan, deprived of warmth and succour.

Greedily, she tugged at his shoulders, reclaimed his mouth, and submitted to a surge of white-hot pleasure as with a groan Paolo took her swollen lips again and plundered the moist interior with explicit thrusts of his tongue.

Suddenly, for Lily, it wasn't enough—not nearly enough.

Heat flamed deep in her pelvis as her restive hands moved from his shoulders to the sides of his face and down, thrusting at the parted sides of his white dinner jacket. Furiously her fumbling fingers worked at the buttons of his shirt, desperate to touch his skin, explore the warmth, the strength of his superb male body.

It wouldn't end with just touching. Lily knew that. But her sense of self-respect, of morality, was vanquished by the sheer power of his erotic hold over her senses. And as he lifted his mouth from hers, removing his jacket with a muffled oath, then caught her to him, burying his face in her hair as he tried to deal with the fastener at the back of the halter strap, his fingers were unsteady.

He was always so in control, but he was losing control now, Lily thought, a wave of tenderness washing over her. Just for tonight his needs came first, and she lifted her hands to release the stubborn clasp. She heard the heady sound of his indrawn breath as the silky fabric slid away to expose the pink-crested peaks of her breasts to his desire-hazed eyes.

'Ah—*bella, bella*! How I want you!' His voice was hoarse as he eased slowly away, putting space between them. 'But my sweet Lily blossom—'

Reckless, fizzing need had her twining her slim arms around his neck, sliding forward and stopping his words as her mouth took his with helpless greed.

In the time it took to take a breath Lily felt him relax. The tension that had taken hold, tautening his powerful body, drained out of him, and now he was kissing her with totally erotic expertise. Her fingers worked with frustrated energy to release the buttons of his shirt, parting the fabric to splay her hands against the hard muscles of his chest, and she was hot with longing as he eased her back against the cushions and took one rosy nipple into his mouth, then moved to the other.

Her head arched back on her slender neck as hot, exquisite sensation flooded every nerve-ending, and he gave a deep groan of male appreciation as she helped him remove her dress with eager, scrabbling hands.

The dress disposed of, Paolo stood and removed the barrier of his clothes with haste, standing before her with the moonlight gleaming on the olive-toned skin that sheathed his male magnificence.

A feverish knot was tightening deep inside her, and with a shaky whimper she held pale, slender arms out to him. As he came to her she knew that her life had been leading up to this one moment of sublime intimacy with the man she loved. Just this one time—a time that would live for ever in her memory. To be treasured. And maybe the memory would surface sometimes for him, making him smile a little as he looked back and remembered…

* * *

'You are everything I ever dreamed of and more,' Paolo murmured with husky sincerity as he slid her shoes onto her dainty feet while dawn rose over the Tuscan hills. He reached for her hands and drew her to her feet. 'You understand *amata mia*, there can be no question now of our not marrying.' He bent his head to place a gentle kiss between her wide, hazy eyes. 'I used no protection. You might be pregnant.'

He felt her shiver. His brows drew together. Surely that was not distaste at the thought of bearing his child? It couldn't be that, could it? Not after the utter perfection of what they'd shared!

Then logic kicked in, and his smile was soft with relief. The dawn air was cold. *She* was cold. He draped his jacket around her shoulders for protection, and slipped a proprietorial arm around her waist as they walked out into the garden.

He hadn't meant it to happen, had meant to show respect and wait until their wedding night. But how could he regret one second of last night?

Worldly-wise, some would say cynical, he had never believed in the fanciful notion of falling in love. But it had happened! His heart swelled until he thought it might burst out of his chest, and his arm tightened around her waist as her pace slowed to a standstill.

Dio mio! How could he not have realised? He'd been growing more in love with her all the time—and his proposal, his manipulations, had had nothing to do with pleasing Mamma, but with pleasing himself! And the first solid indication to enter his thick head had been the violent feelings of white-hot outraged jealousy he'd experienced when he'd seen Orfeo paw her!

Awe at the strength and depth of his feelings for his sweet Lily, for the generous gift of her virginity, made his voice husky as he curved her against the length of his body. 'I was going to take you to Amalfi for a few days— I have a fully staffed villa there. But I've shelved that plan until later, after we're married,' he husked against her hair. 'All my time will be taken with wedding arrangements, making sure it happens as soon as humanly possible.'

Suddenly his hands went to her narrow shoulders, easing her away again. Her melting, exquisitely soft responsiveness had changed to marble-statue rigidity. A cold knot formed inside him. For the first time in his life he felt unsure. He hated the feeling!

'Nothing to say?' His voice sounded harder than he'd expected. He hated himself for that, too!

Lily pulled in a shaky breath. His mention of a possible pregnancy had literally stunned her. His Italian genes would not let him walk away from a child he had sired, and as for letting her raise the child alone, having only visiting rights—well, as far as this macho Italian male was concerned that would be unthinkable, too.

She felt herself shrink within the comforting folds of his white dinner jacket, and her mouth felt as if it were formed out of rock as she asked thinly, 'And if I'm not pregnant?'

Paolo grinned, relief flooding his bloodstream. Was

that all she was worrying about? True, with hindsight he could see that his initial proposal of marriage hadn't been very flattering. All that stuff about pleasing Mamma, when in reality, with patience and the passage of time, he could have handled the flattening of his mother's hopes,

But Lily hadn't known that at the time—hadn't known that he could do whatever he set his mind to. And that included easing himself out of an engagement that had started off as a white lie without causing undue distress to his parent. Maybe now she was suffering from the misapprehension that, having tasted the delights of her body, he had lost interest—he savagely cursed his former reputation—and perhaps would only insist on marriage if an unplanned pregnancy were involved.

'No difference,' he assured her. 'We marry!' And he swept her effortlessly into his arms and carried her back to the villa—rather, Lily thought dazedly, like a warrior bringing home the spoils of war.

He was looking mightily pleased with himself, too, she noted, his midnight hair rumpled, a smile curving that shockingly sensual mouth, golden eyes gleaming with life. He simply took her breath away every time she looked at him. And last night—she would never forget it. Never regret having known such unbelievable ecstasy.

Her eyes filmed with moisture as she remembered that first time, the first of many, when he had come to the barrier—the barrier of her tiny cry of pain—and had stilled, gently withdrawn. She had arched her pelvis, pulsating with frantic need, begging him, 'Don't stop. Don't!'

She would never blame herself for her self-admitted shamelessly wanton behaviour. Never. It had been so beautiful. Limply, she wondered if she could be blamed for taking the next step.

Marrying him only to face heartbreak when the inevitable happened and he moved on, when her novelty value wore off and he sought the delights of some simpering blonde bimbo, satisfied that the woman he'd married to please his mother would be content to stay in the background.

Was that what had happened in his first marriage? Had his wife discovered an infidelity and left him? Had she, as Renata had implied, preferred to overdose rather than face life as a spurned wife?

Dared she risk it?

Could she bear to see her great-aunt and Fiora so bitterly disappointed if she didn't?

Could she face turning down the man she loved to distraction?

CHAPTER ELEVEN

LEAVING the tiny church in the centre of the village that nestled in the valley below the villa, clinging to Paolo's arm, Lily felt totally unreal.

The ceremony had passed like a dream sequence. Her exquisite dress of hand-embroidered ivory silk, the fabulous diamond-encrusted tiara that Fiora had insisted she wear—another family heirloom, apparently—the beautiful bouquet, all seemed to belong squarely in a fairytale rather than to her.

And the tall, incredibly handsome and sexy guy at her side—would he ever truly belong to her?

Stop it, she chided herself. It might not seem real, but you're not dreaming this. It *is* your wedding day and nothing must spoil it!

And she smiled for the photographer.

Her turmoil over whether or not she dared accept his proposal had been brought to an abrupt halt when Paolo had carried her back into the villa in the early morning after the engagement party.

Great-Aunt Edith had been waiting with a face like thunder, her hair coming adrift from its usual tight bun, her stout body enveloped in the sturdy dressing gown she'd had for years.

'And where do you think *you've* been all night?' she'd asked, the stentorian tone pitched at full volume. 'Carla and I insisted Fiora retired to bed hours ago, though the poor dear was fretting. You both disappeared without a word to anyone. Explain yourselves!' she'd demanded, for all the world as if they were naughty children and not adults, one of them a financial legend in the banking world!

Paolo had grinned with a marked lack of repentance, unfazed by one indignant old lady, and remarked smoothly, 'I'm sorry you've been inconvenienced. There really was no need.'

Lily shuddered. Great-Aunt Edith had the strict moral values of a strait-laced Victorian spinster, and what other explanation could there be for a man and a woman creeping in at dawn in such a state of dishevelment!

Carla, hovering at the old lady's elbow, a cup and saucer balanced in one hand, attempted to pour oil on troubled waters by remarking lightly, 'Nothing to get in a state about—what do newly engaged young couples do? I did tell you not to worry.' But that only provided another reason for a trumpeting snort of distaste.

Her back rigid, Edith turned away, waved aside the proffered cup of tea and, with Carla following in her wake, making vague clucking noises, departed.

Lily, wondering why her relative hadn't vented her moral outrage by booming *anticipating marriage!* had collapsed in giggles against Paolo's broad shoulder, and that had been the moment when she'd given in to fate and announced, 'That's done it! We'll have to marry now—otherwise she'll brand me as a fallen woman and make my life a misery!'

Only half joking, she'd realised, as he'd held her even closer and kissed her until she felt her head would spin off her shoulders, that what she'd said was as good an excuse as any for letting her heart rule her head.

During the weeks since then she had seen little of Paolo. The need to tie up business loose ends had kept him either in the Florence head office, or jetting off to meetings in various capital cities, or catching up on arrangements for the forthcoming wedding.

Busy herself with endless fittings, being prodded, tweaked about and told to stand up straight by the flamboyant much-lauded designer Fiora favoured, being consulted over her choice of flowers by the earnest wedding organiser Paolo had engaged, discussing her great-aunt's plans for the sale of her cottage and the transfer of what she called her 'bits and bobs' to Florence, relieved that she'd been forgiven for her bad behaviour, she had still had time to miss him terribly.

She'd also discovered, with a huge and completely unexpected sense of deep disappointment, that she wasn't pregnant.

'You are so beautiful,' Paolo breathed now, as he

handed her into the rear of the limousine that was to take them back to the villa for the small wedding feast, taking both her hands in his as he joined her.

His eyes gleamed like molten gold. She was his now, for all time, and his task of teaching her to love him as he loved her was only just beginning.

'It's the dress,' Lily offered confidingly, knowing he was only saying that to please her, because without fancy trappings she was just ordinary, but loving him for trying to make her feel special.

'Wrong.' The look he gave her sent a gigantic surge of heated sexual awareness through her, bringing back X-rated memories of the night they'd spent together to make her whole body quiver and burn. And when he husked, 'Your naked body is more stunningly beautiful than anything you could possibly wear,' she went bright pink and launched herself at him.

She simply couldn't stop herself, and almost collapsed with sensual overload as he took her willing mouth and kissed her with a devouring hunger that made her vow, there and then, that she would do her utmost, in every possible way, to make sure that she never bored him, never even came close.

Her legs still wobbly from the effect of the sizzling kisses they'd shared on the drive back to the villa, Lily entered the marble-paved, flower-decked hall of the opulent house that was to be her home, walking on air. He might not love her—and she had to be adult about it and accept that he had married her because he'd found it convenient—but it was up to her to wipe his rakish past from her memory and work on making herself *so* convenient he would never think of straying.

The wedding party was small, and security men were discreetly stationed on the driveway. Others patrolled the perimeter on the very slight off-chance that the paparazzi had got wind of a ceremony that had been left deliberately low-key, and Lily, listening to the best man toast the bride and groom, decided that nothing could or would go wrong on her wedding day.

Great-Aunt Edith was beaming beneath the brim of her formidable hat. Lily was glad her much loved relative had chosen to make her home with Fiora. She would have missed her, worried about her being on her own, had she returned to England. And Fiora looked fit as a fiddle, having got the thumbs-up from her consultant, not at all over-tired by the excitement of the wedding.

Her tummy churning with a longing to be alone with her drop-dead handsome new husband, Lily barely touched the delicious food provided by the team of caterers, but drank more than she should of the vintage champagne. She reflected in a rose-tinted glow that even Paolo's cousins seemed to be behaving themselves, and that Renata, dressed down in a plain suit of brown satin, her abundant black hair coiled neatly at the back of her head, must have deliberately chosen not to upstage the bride. Which was really nice of her, because she was stunning and could so easily have done so.

The meal over at last, Lily bestowed a vibrant smile

on her husband, swallowing a giggle because he looked as if he had just taken an icy shower. Cool wasn't in it! She got to her feet, brushing aside the hand he lifted to restrain her, and imparted in a loud whisper, 'Your mother and my great-aunt are getting ready to leave. I'll see them on their way while you chircu—circulate round the rest.' Then she floated away, quite amazed that for once it was she who was dishing out the orders instead of the other way round!

'You're tipsy, child!' Edith accused her as Lily helped her into the car that was to transport them to the Florence apartment.

'It is a very special occasion,' Fiora offered soothingly, 'and I know she doesn't make a habit of it. I believe black coffee helps,' she advised, and Carla, seated in front beside the driver, gave her opinion.

'It's all the excitement.'

Lily, waving violently, even after the car had disappeared, agreed with that.

Excitement at the thrilling prospect of being alone with her fantastically gorgeous brand-new husband had stopped her eating, and whenever she'd lifted her glass for a sip or two of the ice-cold liquid she'd found it topped up to the brim again by one of the over-attentive waiters, with the result that, yes, she did feel a bit floaty.

Forcing herself to walk in a straight line, she headed back inside the villa, determined to make for the kitchen regions and drink gallons of water. But before she could make it there she found her arms taken by Renata, who swung her round and marched her into the empty room that had been Fiora's sitting room during her stay here.

Astonished to find herself hi-jacked, Lily sank unre- sistingly onto the sofa Renata steered her to, her mouth dropping open as she struggled to find something sensible to say when the other woman sank down grace- fully beside her and said, 'Everyone's about to leave, but there's something I want to show you before I go.'

She reached for her slim suede handbag and Lily beamed. Perhaps Paolo's cousin felt bad about the things she'd said on the night of the engagement party and was trying to make friends. If that was the case she'd meet her halfway, because she hated to think there'd be ill-feeling between her and any member of the family she'd married into.

'Oh, lovely—what is it?' she asked, and glanced at the glossy photograph that was placed in her hands, trying not to betray her complete incomprehension.

The studio portrait portrayed a staggeringly beauti- ful young woman. Perfect bone structure, long blonde hair, and what Lily could only describe as really sexy come-to-bed dark brown eyes.

'Solange,' Renata provided. 'Paolo's first wife. She was my best friend.'

'Oh.' Lily didn't know what to say. She passed the photograph back, fighting the urge to rub her fingers on the velvet upholstery of the sofa and rid herself of contamination. That would not only be childish, but insulting too. She knew Paolo had been married before, and didn't like talking about it, so she hadn't ever asked what his first wife had been like. Why the drama queen reaction now, on discovering that she had been so lovely?

'She was French. They met in Paris. She had everything—sophistication, breeding, the natural ability to be the life and soul of every gathering, a promising career on the stage—but she gave it all up when they married.'

Lily shivered. It was far from cold in here, but the look of malice she now detected in the other woman's eyes chilled her. She was beginning to get a thumping headache, but was determined not to throw a wobbly, betray her vulnerability, so she said stiffly, 'As she was your friend you must miss her, and I'm sorry. But my husband's failed marriage has nothing to do with me.'

She would have left the room, but Renata purred, 'Oh, but it has. I'm trying to warn you, you see, do you a favour. I thought you should know what Solange was like. If such a woman couldn't hold his interest for more than a few months, what hope have *you*?'

Lily got awkwardly to her feet. Her legs felt peculiar, as if they didn't belong to her, but she wanted to get out of here, away from this woman who was blatantly doing her level best to poison her marriage before it had properly begun—preying on doubts and fears she already had, did she but know it!

'Wait! There is something else you should see.'

Her heart lurched. Lily's feet refused to move another step. A horrible feeling of nervous tension kept her glued to the spot as Renata came towards her, unfolding a sheet of newsprint.

'An English tabloid—dated one week ago. Look at it.'

Shaking hands accepted the sheet of paper. Lily didn't want to look at it, but couldn't stop herself. Her heart seemed to stop beating. Her entire body felt as if it had closed down as she recognised Paolo exiting one of London's most fashionable and screamingly expensive restaurants.

Caught by the camera flashlight, he was shown with his arm protectively around a leggy blonde who seemed to be trying to climb inside his Savile Row suit. The slick heading asked 'Latest Love for Billionaire Banker?'

Feeling sick with betrayal, Lily thrust the newsprint back at Renata, heard her purr, 'He always goes for blondes—I expect they went back to his hotel, or on to a club and then back…'

Lily walked out, avoiding Paolo and the departing guests by using the staff service staircase. She made it to her room, headed straight into the *en suite* bathroom and was violently sick.

Five minutes later, ashen-faced, she was stone-cold sober. One week before their marriage and fidelity had had no meaning for him.

For the first time Lily gave heartfelt thanks that she wasn't expecting his child.

There would be no children. This marriage was going nowhere. But wallow in her misery she would not. She was tougher than that. She had agreed to marry him knowing his reasons, with her eyes fully open to his faults. That she had let her love for him delude her into thinking that they could grow together, have a stable, happy marriage and create a family, was regrettable— a lesson learned the hard way.

She was sitting on the window seat when he entered the room, already removing his tie. His eyes dazzled her, and he was wearing that heartbreaker smile, and she wondered painfully if she would ever get over the effect he had on her. She wished she'd had time to get out of her wedding dress. But at least she was in control. Totally.

Paolo tossed his jacket over the back of a chair, his mouth quirking as he asked, 'Feeling better now? The champagne went to your head, I think.'

He was advancing. All six foot plus of tall, dark dangerously handsome masculinity.

Her mouth went dry. She looked away. Had to.

'Have I told you how beautiful you are? I want to make love to you. But making love to a drunken woman is the last thing on this earth I would want to do.'

In that he sounded deadly serious. With a fleeting feeling of shame she recalled how she had slurred her words, floated tipsily from the table. If she didn't know what she did she would be apologising for that lapse right now, vowing that it had never happened before and wouldn't happen again.

But she *did* know.

Lily looked at him then, straight into those incredible golden eyes, and watched them go cold as she told him,

'You got what you wanted. A convenient marriage. Fiora's peace of mind. An undemanding wife who will stay in the background, at least for the time being. But I won't sleep with you.'

CHAPTER TWELVE

PAOLO gave her a look of savage condemnation. '*Madonna diavola!* What are you talking about?'

'You heard.' Lily was holding onto her control as if she were clinging to a lifebelt in a raging sea. His leanly handsome face was pale beneath his olive-toned skin, tension lines bracketing his grim mouth. He looked in shock.

Swallowing roughly, she told herself not to give in to the aching need to go to him that claimed every part of her tense body. To hold him, plead a sudden brainstorm or something, beg him to forget what she'd said.

Stoically, she reminded herself of all she had learned. 'The convenient marriage you wanted will stay where it belongs. On paper. I won't share your bed.'

His hard jawline lifted and his eyes narrowed on a fierce demand. 'Why?'

Tell him the truth. Ask what happened between him and Solange. Ask what he was doing with that blonde in London a week ago and listen to his lying explanation. Or maybe he'd tell it as it was, remind her that he didn't love her, didn't believe in it, and regarded himself free to have affairs.

As neither scenario held any appeal whatsoever, she told him the first lie that popped into her head. 'I did what you wanted—got you out of the hole you'd dug for yourself. In return, and until you decide to go for an annulment, I'm owed. I'll live in the lap of luxury, have anything I want. No more getting up at the crack of dawn to wet-nurse a bunch of old people. No more looking at lovely clothes in shop windows and knowing I could never afford them. No more—'

'*Basta!*' he commanded icily, his features like granite. 'I thought you were different from all the others. I regret my mistake.'

Swinging sharply on his heels, his proud, dark head high, he walked from the room.

With that chilling condemnation piercing her heart, Lily burst into uncontrollable tears.

'And where is that son of mine today?' Fiora wanted to know as she dispensed coffee in the lovely high-ceilinged sitting room with its entrancing view over the rooftops of the ancient city to the blue-hazed hills beyond.

'Milan,' Lily answered, a shade too hesitantly—because when he'd given her his itinerary it had been bitten out, as if he begrudged the expenditure of breath wasted in talking to her at all. Relieved to see her hands weren't shaking as she accepted the delicate china cup and saucer, she tacked on, 'For a few days.'

Sitting forward in her wing chair, her head tipped to one side, Fiora said quietly, 'I hope Paolo's not neglecting you.'

'From what he said, I thought you were to honeymoon in Amalfi,' Edith put in, sounding puzzled. 'And I'm sure he told me he intended to pick up his yacht in Cannes to give you a cruise of a lifetime.'

'Life happens,' Lily responded, as airily as she could. 'Business stuff. You'll know all about that.' She directed a stiff smile at her mother-in-law. As the wife of a prominent banker herself, she'd understand that such men always put work before anything else, but all she got was, 'I must speak to him. I have his mobile number. Solange always complained that he was a workaholic.'

Lily's heart squeezed painfully. This was her chance to learn something about his first marriage. She had to take it. 'It was sad—what happened to her—wasn't it?' she prompted.

The sudden rush of adrenalin ebbed away as Fiora merely commented, 'Of course. We shall never know what happened in that marriage. Paolo never speaks of it, and I respect his wishes far too much to ask. It is in the past. He has you now, and a wonderful future to look forward to. Now—' she changed the subject adroitly '—you will stay to lunch?'

'Thank you, but, no.' Lily glanced at her watch. 'I

asked Mario to collect me. I only dropped by to see how the two of you were getting along.'

'Famously!' Edith beamed. 'Like a house on fire! Fiora is trying to teach me Italian—with scant success!—and this morning I heard that my estate agent has received a firm offer for the cottage.'

'When the money comes through I shall take her shopping for some new clothes. She may protest all she likes, but one is never too old to be introduced to Italian style,' Fiora pronounced, busying herself with pouring more coffee. 'I thought via Tornabuoni—I have offered funds, but your dear great-aunt is too stubborn to hear of it! Tomorrow we plan to visit the Boboli Gardens— and, before you start to fuss, I shall take it very easy!'

And so the final half hour of her visit passed without any more awkward questions, any more mention of Fiora contacting her son on the subject of the non-existent honeymoon—or any useful revelations as to the reasons behind the break-up of Paolo's first marriage.

When the car turned into the long driveway Lily said, 'Drop me off here, Mario. I'll walk up to the villa.'

She felt so restless. The feeling had been burning her up ever since her wedding day. Walking quickly to use some of the pent-up nervous energy that made sitting still a torment, she wished, quite uselessly, that she hadn't lied to Paolo about the reasons behind her refusal to make their marriage a real one.

She'd lied to save her pride—believing that it was the only thing left of any value at all to her, hating the thought of coming over as a jealous wife and offering him a big fat clue to the true state of her feelings for him. She was unwilling to let him know she was a world-class idiot, who had self-destructively fallen in love with a man who cynically admitted he didn't know the meaning of the word and who treated women as if they were of as much long-term value as yesterday's newspaper.

So she'd lied. She wished she hadn't.

She'd had little opportunity or encouragement to tell him the truth, though. She'd seen him a scant handful of times since that day. He'd been polite, chillingly so, and so remote. The time they actually spent together was as brief as he could make it, killing dead any hopes she might have had of opening up a meaningful conversation, of making him stay around long enough to listen. It wouldn't make their marriage any more viable, but at least he'd know she wasn't the idle gold-digger she'd made herself out to be.

As she rounded the final bend, perspiring from the heat of the sun and the pace she'd set, she slowed down, frowned. She didn't know who the red sports car in the drive belonged to, but she wasn't in the mood for visitors.

Entering the immense, cool-tiled main hall, she was met by Agata, her kindly features clouded with unease.

'Signorina Renata is here, waiting for you, *signora*. She is in the small salon. She instructed me to bring her a bottle of the *signor*'s best Meursault, and the last time I looked in the bottle was nearly empty.'

Anger rose in a hot tide, but Lily managed to give

a smile of sorts and thank the housekeeper. Renata Venini was the last person she wanted to see. And the small salon was her favourite room, smaller and less grand than the other rooms in the palatial villa. She often sat there herself, finding a peace of sorts for a short while, surrounded by the flowers she'd picked and arranged as something to occupy her long empty day. She hated to think of that wretched woman sullying her space.

Telling herself to cool it, that it was unfair to blame the bearer of bad news, that the other woman had only been telling the truth, Lily pushed open the door and stepped over the threshold.

'So you arrive at last!' Renata was lounging on a cream-upholstered chaise, an empty glass and a bottle containing a few dregs on the table at her side. 'I must say I was surprised to learn you were still here.'

'Really?' Lily wasn't going to give an inch until she knew why Paolo's cousin was really here. She just hoped, desperately, that it wasn't to give her more evidence of his womanising.

Renata yawned, closely examining her scarlet-tipped fingernails as if for flaws, obviously unimpressed by Lily's attempt at cool. 'Absolutely. Do you know—' she leant over and poured the last of the wine into her glass '—this used to be Solange's favourite room? For the view of the fountain and the roses—so pretty.'

One more thing spoiled for her! Grinding her teeth to stop herself from telling the other woman to sling her hook, Lily had to literally force herself to remain calm. 'Why are you here?'

'Friendly visit. As I told you, I wanted to know if you were still here, or if you'd done the sensible thing and returned to wherever it is you came from. And how *is* dear cousin Paolo?'

There was nothing friendly about this woman where Lily was concerned. She might have been telling the truth, but it had been done with malice and spite. 'He is well.'

'You know that for sure?' A trill of laughter. 'How can you when he's never here? Oh, don't look so surprised! I have no spy among your servants. They are all too loyal to his lordship to tell me anything. But did you know that one of your under-gardeners is having an operation for something or other?'

Lily, standing firmly where she was, just inside the door, said nothing. Old Carlo Barzini was recovering from a gall bladder operation. She had had fruit and a cured ham delivered to their house in the village, but she wasn't about to enlighten Renata, who wouldn't be interested in any case.

'His simple-minded son—Beppe, I think he is called—doesn't understand this tribal loyalty,' Renata went on. 'He tells me my cousin has hardly been seen here since the wedding.' She emptied her glass and heaved herself upright. 'Up to his old tricks. Keep little wifey locked up at home and swan about earning lots more money to spend on whatever leggy blonde happens to be flavour of the month.'

'I think you should go.' Lily was breaking up inside, but she wasn't going to show it.

'I'm sure you do. However, I am too tired to drive, so I'll find a nice comfy bed and rest awhile. This is Venini property, after all. And I am a Venini by birth, not by borrowed name.' She headed none too steadily for the door, brushing past Lily, rigid with rage. 'Oh, and warn the housekeeper that I may be staying on for dinner.'

Underwhelmed by that prospect, Lily screwed her eyes shut to stop herself crying, and swallowed the painful lump in her throat. Spinning on her heels, she sped out of the house. Renata had touched a raw nerve when she'd said that stuff about 'little wifey' being locked up at home.

She felt like a prisoner. If she wanted to go anywhere Mario drove her. If she wandered through the extensive grounds one of the gardeners always seemed to be around.

Fuming now, she stood on the gravelled forecourt. She had to escape—just for a little while. To be on her own and think. Things couldn't go on the way they were.

Could she pin Paolo down long enough to ask him to go for an immediate annulment? Telling him that she wanted nothing from him would at least take away the bad taste left by the way she'd lied about enjoying the wealth he had to offer.

And surely the break-up wouldn't affect Fiora and Edith? She'd seen for herself how comfortable they were with each other, had listened to their plans for future outings and spending sprees.

As for her—what she'd do, how she'd manage when she got back to England—well, she'd think of something.

Stress made her muscles tight, her breathing painfully difficult, and hot tears stung behind her eyes. But she wasn't going to cry. All this was her own fault. No one else was to blame. She'd had plenty of warning about what he was like, but she'd ignored it. He'd told her he didn't love her, didn't *do* love, that their marriage would be 'convenient', and she'd ignored that too!

After one night of ecstatically beautiful sex, and discovering her love for him, she'd decided that the marriage would work, that he would stay faithful to her. Well, she'd been wrong.

Keyed up to the point of explosion, she determined to get away from the environs of the beautiful villa that had come to feel like a prison—even if she found an army of Paolo's staff trailing after her. Then she noticed for the first time that Renata had left her keys in the ignition of her scarlet sports car.

The fleeting thought that the other woman wouldn't be needing it until she'd slept off the effects of the wine she'd drunk was all it took before she was in the driving seat, gunning the engine, and speeding down the drive.

The Ferrari scorched to a halt. Paolo exited, his long legs carrying him at speed towards the main door of the villa that seemed to be sleeping peacefully in the late-afternoon sun.

When Fiora had called his mobile that morning he'd

known something had to be very wrong. She never phoned him while he was working except in an emergency. The last time it had happened had been when she'd begged him to come home because Antonio had been involved in that dreadful accident.

Superficially she'd been asking why he and Lily weren't on their planned honeymoon. He'd neglected to tell her that there was no point in a honeymoon if the bride wouldn't have anything to do with the groom, and fobbed her off waiting for the real reason for her call.

'Lily came on a short visit this morning. She's only just left. There's something wrong, and you must forget you run a banking empire and do something about it. She's lost weight. Edith and I both noticed it. And her eyes are so sad. All those sunny smiles are missing. She didn't say so, but we are both sure she is unhappy. You may be a powerful man, my son, but you are also a husband who is making a very big mistake in leaving his new bride alone to pine.'

His strong face clenched, he'd ended the call, made his apologies, and strode out of the meeting he'd been chairing.

A big mistake. Since his marriage to Solange he'd made sure he never made mistakes, but his gut feeling told him he had this time. Weight loss and sad eyes didn't gel with the type of woman who admitted she'd married a man solely for what she could get out of him.

She wasn't in the suite of rooms she'd used since he'd first manipulated her into coming here.

The way she'd destroyed their marriage before it had begun had shocked him, hurt his pride, hurt his heart—the heart that had finally learned how to love. So, rather than display his shocking vulnerability where she was concerned, he'd removed himself.

He should have stuck around, found out what had turned his sweet Lily into an avaricious monster, discovered if she'd been telling the truth or using that preposterous statement to cover something else. Instead he'd buried himself in work—always his refuge.

Grinding his teeth, he clattered down the stairs to summon his staff and ask them for his wife's whereabouts. Then he noticed the empty bottle and solitary glass through the open doorway to the small salon.

His blood ran cold, then scaldingly hot. Lily rarely drank, and never to excess. But she'd been tipsy on champagne on their wedding day. His darkly handsome features tightened. Had she got a taste for the stuff? Hence the solitary glass and empty bottle?

A movement on the periphery of his vision galvanised him. The main door still stood open, as he'd left it, and Beppe was trundling a wheelbarrow across the forecourt. Not the most reliable source of information, but as everyone else seemed to have disappeared he'd do.

Two minutes later he was back behind the wheel of the Ferrari. Yes, Beppe had seen the *signora*. She had driven a car away very fast. No, Mario had not been with her.

Paolo's heart was beating despite the iron band that seemed to be squeezing it to pulp. No point in going to see which car was missing from the many vehicles garaged in the old stable block. With that much wine inside her she wasn't fit to ride a tricycle!

When he discovered who had allowed her to have the ignition keys, he would kill the idiot!

That he had no idea where she'd been heading didn't matter a damn. He would find her. He had to.

Ferocious tension held him as he sent the powerful car hurtling round bends, up a steep gradient that led to a spectacular viewpoint, much loved by visitors to the area. Cresting the rise, he saw her leaning against the safety barrier. In the same moment he recognised his cousin's poky sports model.

Out of the Ferrari in no time, covering the distance to where she was in two seconds flat, he took her arm, pulled her round to face him and lashed out, '*Madre di Dio!* What do you think you're doing?'

Her heart thumping against her ribcage with shock, Lily was speechless for several seconds as she stared, wide-eyed, into his tautly grim features. She'd heard a car screech to a standstill and cursed whoever it was who had come to spoil her solitude just when she was getting things sorted out in her head.

Pulling herself together with an effort, she narrowed her eyes at him and said, 'And hello to you, too!'

He dealt her a chilling glance. 'This is not the time for sarcasm. With the amount of alcohol you have in your blood *anything* could have happened!'

Her face bone-white, eyes wide with incomprehension, Lily searched his unforgiving features and wondered just what it was about this arrogant, bullying, congenitally unfaithful man that made her love him so very much. She must have had a common-sense bypass, she decided mournfully. Then she remembered what he'd said, and said hotly, 'I have *not* been drinking. Why assume I have?'

Very much on her high horse, she snatched her arm away from his grasp and rubbed the tender spot where his fingers had dug into her flesh.

'On the evidence of a single glass and an empty wine bottle,' he returned heavily. He expelled what felt like solidified air from his lungs. 'When Beppe told me you'd taken off behind the wheel of a car—' Dark colour flooded his fantastic cheekbones as he admitted, 'I was worried.'

Lily's soft mouth tightened as the penny dropped. He must have called in at the villa, seen the empty wine bottle and decided she'd gone joy-riding in a drunken stupor.

Pulling herself up to her negligible height, she put him straight. 'I didn't drink that stuff. Renata did. She was there when I got back from visiting in Florence. She's crawled into some bed or other to sleep it off. I took her car because I wanted to go some place to think—away from my keepers!'

There was relief in his roughened tone as he frowned down at her. 'Renata and over-indulgence adds up. What is *she* doing here?'

Determined not to answer that right now, Lily said

thinly, 'We need to talk about the future. We can't go on like this.'

'Not here.' The need to straighten stuff out and not hide his head and his breaking heart in his work was what had brought him back, shattering all speed records. He paced to his cousin's car, locked it and pocketed the keys, explaining tersely, at Lily's gabbled objection, 'Someone can drive her here to collect it when she's sobered up. Right now, I don't trust you out of my sight.'

His profile was so grim as he drove them back through the twilight that Lily didn't dare bring up the vexed subject of their marriage and the annulment thereof. She was still biting her tongue to stop the rapidly piling up words from spilling out when, with a hand firmly on the small of her back, he propelled her into the now brightly lit great hall, bawling for Agata and informing the astonished woman that she was to hold dinner until he informed her they were ready. Should Signorina Renata surface she was to wait in the staff quarters until he could deal with her. No interruptions were to be permitted, on pain of instant dismissal.

'You are such a bully!' Lily condemned breathily as he ushered her into the small salon and closed the door with pointed firmness behind them.

'Only when my patience has reached its outer limits,' he came back. The scowl he wore now was pretty fierce, but he didn't scare her. She'd stood up to him in the past. She could do it again.

But first she needed a moment to gather her thoughts.

The concise sentence that encapsulated her need for a speedy annulment, the advancement of enough funds to buy an air ticket back to England, had somehow flown out of her head, and she needed to sound businesslike, not babble.

Walking to the window, she gazed out. The fountain was always lit up as night fell, and the beds of roses that surrounded the stone basin were gorgeous. She would miss this lovely house when she was gone.

And she would mourn for what she and Paolo could have had.

'Come here, Lily.' The instruction was softly couched. A tremor shook her slight frame. She turned slowly, reluctant, now it had come right down to it, to face the final death knell of their marriage.

But she had never been short of courage, had she?

Watching her, standing so straight, Paolo felt as if he were coming apart. Fiora was right. She had lost weight, and she looked terminally tired. Somehow he had messed up—big-time. It was up to him to get to the bottom of this. He wanted to go to her, take her hand, lead her to the sofa he had parked himself on, but knew he couldn't. She clearly didn't want him touching her.

'Right.' He cut to the chase, getting to his feet but not moving closer. 'You married me, and yet you deliberately set out to destroy our marriage by refusing to share my bed. It occurs to me that is grounds for an annulment, which would mean you wouldn't be entitled to anything. And yet you claim to have married me solely for a lavish lifestyle,' he expounded with clinical precision. 'It doesn't make sense.'

In a shocking state of agitation, Lily twisted her hands together, happy that he'd seen through her stupid lie, yet feeling a dreadful fool for having told it in the first place.

'It was a pathetic lie,' she admitted. 'I really don't want anything from you—you've already done masses for the charity—'

'Then why did you say it?' he demanded, with no patience whatsoever. 'You had to have a reason, and nattering on about what I've put into Life Begins isn't doing it for me!'

Her troubled face crumpled. She couldn't bear this. In a rush to get it over with, she blurted, 'It's my fault! I shouldn't have agreed to marry you. Not knowing what I did.'

'That being?'

His voice sounded as if it had been filtered through ice. Telling herself not to be faint-hearted, Lily launched in. 'This is going to sound really dreadful. And I don't suppose you can help yourself.' In a pause for breath she was sure she could hear his teeth grinding, so she pushed rapidly on. 'You get bored with women very easily. Even when you're engaged or married to them. And you can't resist blondes and playing away with them. I knew all this stuff, but when I went and fell in love with you I thought I could make you like me enough to stay faithful.'

Realising she'd let the cat out of the bag, Lily fell into

an appalled silence. Paolo was staring at her as if he couldn't believe his ears and she couldn't blame him—because he wouldn't want to hear what he would classify as sentimental twaddle.

'What?'

He was advancing towards her. Slowly. If she hadn't known better she would have said his state was trance-like. But macho Italian males didn't do trances.

'I—er—well, actually it was a piece in a London paper. A photo taken of you coming out of a fancy restaurant with some blonde glued to you. A week before our wedding!'

Much to her horror, her eyes welled with tears. She was coming over as such a wimp!

'Say that again, *mi amore*.' He took both her hands.

Flustered, Lily repeated, 'A week before our wedding.' She wondered if he was checking dates to verify which blonde in particular he'd been seeing, and wished he wasn't touching her because that made life so very difficult.

'No.' Wired as he was, he had to take this calmly. 'What you said about falling in love with me.'

Her face flushed with embarrassment. He really was something else! Going for her weak spot, gloating! Disregarding what she'd said about that blonde as if his two-timing behaviour was something she had no right to mention!

But there was no wriggling out of it. Not when those golden eyes seemed to be reaching right into her soul.

Swallowing thickly, she bit the bullet. 'I'll be the first to admit it was stupid, but I really fell for you. It sort of grew on me, and I knew if we had a normal marriage I'd get so hurt I wouldn't be able to stand it.'

His fingers tightened on her hands as he drew her closer to him. And he said unevenly, 'I will never hurt you, *cara*. I love you far too much!'

'You don't have to say that,' Lily mumbled disconsolately, then decided she was being pretty dumb—because why would he say that if he didn't mean it? Unless, of course, he was thinking about the effect the sudden break-up would have on his mother? 'You don't *do* love,' she reminded him, trying not to notice the fizz of excitement that claimed her at the contact with his lean, sexy body.

'True.' His lips were on her hair. 'Until I met you. Like you, it sort of grew on me.' His mouth had moved to the lobe of her ear. 'I was in love with you long before I recognised the condition—not having had the experience before.'

Her heart was singing. His lips trailed down the side of her neck. She was rapidly reaching the point where she'd believe anything he said. Wrenching her head away from the indescribably sweet temptation of his lips, she said, with a shake in her voice, 'That's not true! You were engaged once. You must have thought you loved her. And then you got married. You must have felt something for her—you never mention her. And what about that blonde you were with that night?'

'Ah.' His grin was unashamedly rueful. 'We have to go through the serious stuff before I get to kiss my wife. Pity. I was enjoying myself for the first time since you banned me from your bed!'

Forgiving him, because she'd been feeling just the same, she allowed him to lead her to one of the twin sofas, biting on the corner of her mouth as she registered that he was looking decidedly serious now.

'Since when have you started reading that brand of gutter press?'

Silence. Lily bit down harder. As it was, Paolo didn't rate his cousins. She didn't want to give him cause to despise them.

'Tell me, Lily,' he asked gently. 'Someone must have shown you the piece. Was it Renata? I can't think of anyone else capable of such spite.' When she nodded uncomfortably, he said soberly, 'She holds a grudge because of what happened with my first wife. She introduced me to Solange. She was her closest friend and on/off bed partner—although I didn't get to know that until much later. I'm certain that Renata thought she'd get her hands on some of the family wealth through Solange. Any chance of that vanished when I ended the marriage.'

'Why did you?' Lily sat up very straight. Suddenly she knew she could believe him implicitly. He'd already been very open on a subject even his own mother said he never talked about.

'I made an error of judgement. For the second time in my life.' His fine eyes darkened. 'Believe me, it's tough to have to admit that. The first was when I got engaged to Maria. I was nineteen, she was six years older, with a modelling career that I guess, with hindsight, was going downhill. She was glamorous; I was flattered. Cocky, if you like! My parents disapproved, but I thought a mixture of flattery and rampaging hormones was love. I soon discovered it wasn't, and the only thing that hurt was my pride when I overheard her telling a friend that she'd landed a meal ticket for life.'

'Oh, my!' Lily's eyes widened until they almost filled her face. 'Poor you—you must have been shattered,' she breathed, unable to imagine anyone wanting to marry him for his money when he had so much else to offer.

'Not so you'd notice.' He grinned at her, then sobered. 'It made me wary, and no bad thing. Then, years later, when I was introduced to Solange, I'd reached a point in my life when I thought it was time to settle down long-term, start a family. I made a list of pros and cons, and the pros outweighed the cons.'

'How very businesslike!'

A dark eyebrow rose. 'I was still being wary, remember? To cut a long story short, she said she was madly in love with me. Said she wanted my children, the whole bag. She was beautiful, classy, witty. Suitable. We were married after a very short engagement. On honeymoon I discovered that she was an alcoholic and a drug addict—something she'd cleverly hidden from me. I tried to get her to admit she needed help, but whenever I mentioned it she threw a screaming tantrum, flounced out, and usually ended up at some wild party, returning some time the next day, barely able to stand, vowing it would never happen again. But it always did. In the end I lost patience—told her to get help for her addiction or say goodbye to our marriage. Frankly, by that stage I was beyond caring. I sometimes think I should have tried harder. If I'd really loved her I would have tied her up and delivered her bodily to a clinic with the knowledge and experience to deal with such things. But I didn't love her.'

Lily took his hand, hating to see him blaming himself for something he hadn't been able to control. His fingers tightened around hers as he went on flatly, 'She chose to walk out and went to Renata. It was then I discovered they'd been having a sexual relationship for years. I washed my hands of her. Her lifestyle was out of control, and soon she died—an accidental overdose.'

Lily wrapped her arms around him. He must have had a horrible time. No wonder he'd bawled her out earlier. He must have thought she'd taken to the bottle, that history was repeating itself.

'Well, I love you to bits,' she vowed. 'And I don't drink more than the odd glass socially, and I don't want your money, and you're stuck with me—'

'Aren't you forgetting something?' He tilted her chin and brushed his mouth lightly over her luscious lips. 'The identity of the blonde I wined and dined?'

Coming back down to earth with a bump, Lily tilted her head consideringly. He'd said he loved her, and she believed him, so 'Tell me her name and I'll go and kill her!' She giggled.

'That would be a pity. She's an excellent head of futures. I was running on a tight schedule—planning to take my wife on an extended honeymoon—and dinner was the only slot I could find in my diary. A working dinner. My days of indulging in short-term, no-strings soulless affairs with bimbos are over—have been for some time. And there were never as many as the tabloids credited me with. I've fallen madly, irrevocably in love with a real woman, and right now I want to take her to bed and get this marriage up and running. Agreed?'

'Not very romantically put—but, yes, I agree.' She gave him a tender smile and he gave her a wicked one back.

'Romantic I can do. Later.' And he marched her into the hall where Agata was hovering, looking at a loss.

'Is Renata about?'

'*Si, signor.* In the kitchen. She has eaten, but is growing—' she sought suitably tame words '—a little annoyed.'

'Good.' He tossed the car keys over. 'Give her these and ask Mario if he will drive her home. She can collect her car tomorrow, when she's sober. It is parked on the side of the road by the viewpoint, a couple of kilometres away. Mario will know where I mean.'

At that he gave Lily the sort of smile that had always made her fizzle and melt, swept her up in his arms and headed for the stairs.

Later he was very romantic indeed. Lily decided she'd never have anything to complain about for the rest of her life, and made a staunch vow that he wouldn't, either.

HARLEQUIN *Presents*

**Harlequin Presents brings you
a brand-new duet by star author**

Sharon Kendrick

THE GREEK BILLIONAIRES' BRIDES

Possessed by two Greek billionaire brothers

Alexandros Pavlidis always ended his affairs before
boredom struck. After a passionate relationship with
Rebecca Gibbs, he never expected to see her again.
Until she arrived at his office—pregnant, with twins!

Don't miss

THE GREEK TYCOON'S
CONVENIENT WIFE,

on sale July 2008

www.eHarlequin.com   HP12744

HARLEQUIN *Presents*

Royal Brides

Lucy Monroe

*delivers two more books from
her irresistible Royal Brides series.*

Billionaire businessman Sebastian Hawk and
Sheikh Amir are bound by one woman: Princess Lina.
Sebastian has been hired to protect Lina—but all he
wants to do is make her his. Amir has arranged to marry
her—but it's his virgin secretary he wants in his bed!

Two men driven by desire—who will they
make their brides?

FORBIDDEN: THE BILLIONAIRE'S VIRGIN PRINCESS

Sebastian Hawk is strong, passionate
and will do anything to claim the woman
he wants. Only, Lina is forbidden to him
and promised to another man....

Available July 2008

Don't miss
HIRED: THE SHEIKH'S SECRETARY MISTRESS

On sale August 2008

www.eHarlequin.com

HP12739

THE BOSS'S MISTRESS

Out of the office…and into his bed

These ruthless, powerful men are used
to having their own way in the office—
and with their mistresses they're also
boss in the bedroom!

Don't miss any of our fantastic stories
in the July 2008 collection:

#13 THE ITALIAN
TYCOON'S MISTRESS
by CATHY WILLIAMS

#14 RUTHLESS BOSS, HIRED WIFE
by KATE HEWITT

#15 IN THE TYCOON'S BED
by KATHRYN ROSS

#16 THE RICH MAN'S
RELUCTANT MISTRESS
by MARGARET MAYO

www.eHarlequin.com

HPE0708

HARLEQUIN Presents

THE SICILIANS

They seek passion—at any price!

A sizzling trilogy by

Carole Mortimer

Two brothers and their cousin are all of
Sicilian birth—and all have revenge in mind
and romance in their destinies!

THE SICILIAN'S RUTHLESS MARRIAGE REVENGE

Sicilian billionaire Cesare Gambrelli blames the Ingram
dynasty for the death of his beloved sister. The beautiful
daughter of the Ingram family, Robin, is now the object
of his revenge by seduction....

On sale July 2008

Don't miss

AT THE SICILIAN'S
COUNT'S COMMAND

On sale August 2008

www.eHarlequin.com

HP12742

REQUEST YOUR FREE BOOKS!

2 FREE NOVELS PLUS 2 FREE GIFTS!

PASSION GUARANTEED SEDUCTION

YES! Please send me 2 FREE Harlequin Presents® novels and my 2 FREE gifts (gifts are worth about $10). After receiving them, if I don't wish to receive any more books, I can return the shipping statement marked "cancel". If I don't cancel, I will receive 6 brand-new novels every month and be billed just $4.05 per book in the U.S. or $4.74 per book in Canada, plus 25¢ shipping and handling per book and applicable taxes, if any*. That's a savings of close to 15% off the cover price! I understand that accepting the 2 free books and gifts places me under no obligation to buy anything. I can always return a shipment and cancel at any time. Even if I never buy another book, the two free books and gifts are mine to keep forever.

106 HDN ERRW 306 HDN ERRL

Name	(PLEASE PRINT)
Address	Apt. #
City	State/Prov. Zip/Postal Code

Signature (if under 18, a parent or guardian must sign)

Mail to the Harlequin Reader Service:
IN U.S.A.: P.O. Box 1867, Buffalo, NY 14240-1867
IN CANADA: P.O. Box 609, Fort Erie, Ontario L2A 5X3

Not valid to current subscribers of Harlequin Presents books.

Want to try two free books from another line?
Call 1-800-873-8635 or visit www.morefreebooks.com.

* Terms and prices subject to change without notice. N.Y. residents add applicable sales tax. Canadian residents will be charged applicable provincial taxes and GST. This offer is limited to one order per household. All orders subject to approval. Credit or debit balances in a customer's account(s) may be offset by any other outstanding balance owed by or to the customer. Please allow 4 to 6 weeks for delivery. Offer available while quantities last.

Your Privacy: Harlequin Books is committed to protecting your privacy. Our Privacy Policy is available online at www.eHarlequin.com or upon request from the Reader Service. From time to time we make our lists of customers available to reputable third parties who may have a product or service of interest to you. If you would prefer we not share your name and address, please check here. ☐

HP08